The Inheritance: A Fogpoint Harbor Novel

First Printing, 2023

Imprint: Imagine Nation

Imagine Nation

Chenoa, IL 61726

AuthorJenniferLush@gmail.com

Chapter One
Ocean View

"RECALCULATING," THE voice from the dash repeated. "Make legal U-turn."

It had been repeating the same message several times now, and Kat considered shutting it down. If she wasn't concentrating so hard on the winding road, more specifically watching for bear and moose around each curve, she would turn it off until she found the road she wanted to take. There might not be as much likelihood of encountering a large animal so near the coast, but she wasn't an expert on the area. She had been a child the last time she was in these parts, but there was a memory that was reluctant to reveal itself fully to her about the wildlife. Either she had seen these magnificent creatures, or she had been told to keep an eye out for them. If the latter were the case, it could've been talk to keep her occupied and sharpen her imagination. It was better to play it safe with the animals that may or may not be in the woods until she knew for sure what to expect.

There wasn't a lot of time left until the sun began to set, so she pushed the car as fast as she dared given her surroundings.

She had hoped to drive the coastal road into town. That was one memory she had never forgotten. According to the map she had studied online before leaving home, the right turn she took at the last intersection before the interstate would lead her straight to it. She hoped it wouldn't be too long until her GPS caught on to what she was doing and updated the route.

This town had crossed her mind often in the twenty or so years since her last visit, but she had never expected to make a trip out this way again. There were so many questions now, mysteries that would likely never be solved. There were countless reasons for her to make the trip back to Fogpoint Harbor after all these years. One hundred thousand of them to be exact. The most compelling one was trying to discover the truth.

She had hoped to find something in the old Victorian house, letters, or a diary perhaps, that would put her on the right course to finding answers. Maybe there was someone in town who knew her well enough and held her aunt's confidence who could help, but she knew that was unlikely. Even with the innocence of childhood, she had been able to recognize that her aunt didn't quite fit in with others and preferred her solitude. There was some secrets, she was afraid, that had already gone to the grave.

"In one mile, turn left," the voice from the dash told her.

Kat breathed a sigh of relief, but not because her GPS had finally sorted itself out. Her sense of direction was impeccable, and she would have found the small coastal town even without having memorized the map she had looked at before leaving home. The solace she felt from hearing those words came from knowing she would make it to the ocean before the sun set.

When she hit the last straightaway before the T-intersection of the scenic coastal drive that would take her to Fogpoint, the ocean appeared suddenly. It hadn't been visible until now except for a few small patches of shimmering blue which occasionally could be seen through the dense trees. It loomed before her spread wide, unbroken by landmarks or boats. It looked as though she could drive straight into the water, and her stomach flopped from the alarming sensation.

This is what she had been waiting to see most of all. She pulled up to the stop sign and put her car in park. This is where she would sit until she had her fill of the view or until an impatient local came up behind her, blaring the horn. The hurry wasn't to reach Fogpoint, but simply to make it to the ocean before daylight had completely faded from the sky.

Of all her childhood memories here, the ocean was her favorite. She hadn't been a strong swimmer and still wasn't. The water was never allowed to reach higher than her ankles for her own sense of safety, but she had loved sitting on the beach watching the waves.

As a child staring out at the vast ocean as far as she could see, she got her first sense that the world was so much bigger than she had ever realized and wondered about everything the world offered that she would never know. That was the type of child she had been, the type of person she still was. Her mind was like a sponge always absorbing everything around her, always seeing more than meets the eye, and always questioning everything.

The waves of the ocean entranced her, and soon they enveloped her in the sensation of being swept off to sea even though she was buckled into the driver's seat of her Escape.

It caught her off guard, and she lost her balance, causing her to flail her arms out as if she were falling. Kat chuckled remembering how she used to try to force this effect while balancing on a piece of drift wood at the beach. When she was no older than five or six, she based her determination on whether it had been a good day on how many times she felt just like this.

No trip to the beach was complete without a stop at The Shack. Her aunt would indulge her whatever she'd like as a reward for behaving. "Cherry snow cone," was Kat's constant order.

Aunt Dot would throw her head back and laugh. "Are you sure?"

They'd sit at a table near the front of the waterside shop and eat their treats before returning to the parking lot. Her aunt would lick the sides of her ice cream sandwich routinely to salvage it from melting away in the hot sun. "You sure love those snow cones," she would say.

Kat would nod and devour her flavored ice. Fogpoint was the only place she was able to get them. Her parents had ice cream on occasion, but never these.

Her aunt was old even then, but thinking back, the images Kat's mind stirred up painted her younger than she really was. It had to be her youthful spirit that skewed the images in a better light. When her mom lied to her about her aunt's death, Kat was surprised to learn Dot was actually her great-aunt, a whole generation older than her mother. She'd always thought they were the same age with her mom maybe even being a tad older.

It was their actions she based the assumption on more than

anything. Her mom was always too tired, too busy. It was rare for them to do anything more than walk to the park a couple blocks from the house where her mom would sit on a bench and occasionally talk to one of the other parents. It was always one of the fathers which Kat didn't think much about until after her own father died. As an adult, she wondered when her mom started cheating on him.

Kat entertained herself at home mostly unless her father was off work to keep her imagination busy. There were a couple kids in the neighborhood near her age, but they were both boys who didn't like having a girl tag along. It had been quite lonely except for her visits to the coast.

Aunt Dot never seemed to run out of steam. They'd spend the morning at the beach, walk all over Fogpoint after returning home, and hike through the trees behind her aunt's house pretending anything from a wild animal safari to pirates entering the cove. At the end of each day, her aunt would still be up for a game of indoor hide and seek until Kat was wore out and ready for bed. In the morning, they'd do it all again.

It seemed like it had been only minutes since she pulled up to the stop sign, but the light from the sky was darkening. The clock on her dash proved she'd been there close to an hour watching the water and letting her mind roam freely. She needed to head to Fogpoint as much as she didn't want to leave from that spot. The ocean would still be there tomorrow.

Carelessly, she put the car in drive and pulled away without checking for traffic. There hadn't been a single vehicle the entire time she sat there lost in her own thoughts. Her car hadn't moved more than a couple feet before she slammed on the brakes to avoid hitting the jeep careening down the coastal road, speeding high above the posted limit. The other driver honked at her and yelled something her way she didn't catch, but she got the gist of what he was saying.

The manila envelope laying on the passenger seat fell to the floorboard, scattering the contents. Kat reached down, picking it all up and laying it haphazardly with the envelope. She'd go through it at the house to put everything in order. When she tossed it on the seat again, she noticed a picture still laying on the floor of her and her aunt. She must've been around seven years old when it was taken.

It had been a long forgotten memory until she saw the photograph the day she met with the lawyer to discuss the estate. The details of that day came back clearly and were still refreshed in her mind. Aunt Dot's friend Maggie had taken the picture, but Kat had never seen it until a couple months ago. When she was a child, the option to delete if you weren't happy with it and try again wasn't widely available yet. Film was sent off for processing unless you wanted to pay the ridiculous fees to receive your photos in an hour. It was never an hour either, but by the end of the day, you'd have the pictures in your hand. Most of them blurry, out of focus, and your subject's eyes would be closed. This one had turned out perfectly. It was probably the best photo of her aunt she had and likely the only one of the two of them together.

It wasn't the first time she met Maggie, but their interactions had been brief and rare. Maggie had been close to her mom's age and usually visited with her aunt once or twice while Kat was there. To her knowledge, she was the only real friend her aunt had. No one else had ever been over throughout any of Kat's visits to Fogpoint.

Maggie was the only person Kat was aware of who might be able to help her unravel the mysteries surrounding the lies she had been told. If only she had more to go on than a first name, she would have better luck in tracking her down. It wasn't going to deter her. If the answers weren't in her aunt's house, she'd knock on every door in Fogpoint until she found her, or found someone who could point her in the right direction.

Kat pulled in the drive to the house. It was the last house on a dead end street, sitting high enough to overlook the town and the water below. The incline of the driveway was noticeable, but not too steep. It looked almost exactly as it had during Kat's last visit nearly twenty years ago. The only difference was the drive had been paved and was much smoother than the gravel it replaced.

She picked up the papers littered on the passenger seat and shuffled them together, tapping the bottoms of the pages to neaten the pile. Tomorrow she'd go through them and see what she needed and what could be stored away forever in a tote marked, 'Important.' Her aunt's will, copies of the death certificate, and various account information and deeds were all there. Dorothy Libby's life had been reduced to one manila envelope.

A brief flutter of panic hit her before she remembered she had added the house key to the chain dangling from the ignition. Leaning over far enough to have the gear shift dig into her ribs, she picked up the photo off the floor of the car and stared at it. Her eyes watered, but she refused to cry. She grieved her aunt when she was ten. There was no sense in rehashing those emotions over years lost. She didn't tuck the picture into the envelope with the rest of the paperwork. It would go on her old nightstand tonight propped against the lamp until she could buy a frame for it. This was her own housewarming gift for her new home as temporary as it was.

Chapter Two
Unexpected Hoarding

THE OLD VICTORIAN HOUSE looked smaller than she remembered. It was still large and exquisite, but it didn't have the same mansion feel it gave her as a child. Everything has a grander appeal when you're little. The house sat on the property at the end of a dead end street. There was a bit of an incline on the driveway up to the house. As a child, she never noticed how foreboding it loomed, resting on the hill overlooking the town below.

Behind the house, passed the patio and yard less than a mile into the trees, the cliffs began. It had been off limits to her unless her aunt was with her. The ocean was hard to miss during the day, but even at night, lights reflected off the water providing a clear landmark warning people of its location. They'd sometimes walk near the cliffs, but not too close, enjoying the view of the cove which only they had access to see.

She stood on the porch with one suitcase in her hand as she had every time she arrived in Fogpoint, but the difference this time was the car full of belongings she'd have to unload in the morning. This time she wouldn't be leaving at the end of the summer, but rather after one full year. There were a couple lights shining through the windows. The utilities had been turned on in her name almost two weeks ago when she prepared for the move, but she didn't consider whether everything was off in the house before she did it.

Kat fished the rather ridiculous set of connected key rings from her purse. It would be a guessing game to determine what all the keys unlocked if they even all still had a purpose. There were fourteen key chains connected together with thirty-nine keys of varying styles. The one to the front door had been marked with a piece of blue masking tape and was on a separate ring when she received the keys from the lawyer. Kat had added it to the key ring for her car, but what the rest of the keys unlocked would have to be figured out and labeled somehow.

When she opened the door, the familiar scent of jasmine overtook her like her aunt was welcoming her home. The house was saturated in the scent, and it warmed Kat who hadn't thought about it in years. It was harder to grow this far north, but not impossible. Her aunt loved everything jasmine from perfumes, soaps, air fresheners, potpourri sachets, and of course, the flower. All the florists in town had kept her aunt in good supply because her aunt couldn't even grow a weed if her life had depended on it.

The aroma took her back, and she was filled with a sadness she hadn't expected to face. She had grieved her aunt as a child. The first couple summers after the news were the hardest. It was the time she would've spent with Aunt Dot on the coast. As time passed, her grief lessened, and she was thankful for the time she had with her great aunt.

It came as quite a shock when she discovered her aunt had

only recently passed away at the age of ninety-four. Kat felt cheated. There were almost twenty years she missed out on having a connection to her roots in addition to her mom who refused to talk about family history. To make it worse, there was no one left to explain why she had been lied to about Aunt Dot, or why her aunt had never tried to contact her.

It was one thing when she was a child because her mom could've stopped any attempts her aunt might have made. She was twenty-nine now which meant there had been plenty enough time for her aunt to track her down as an adult, but she never did. The last five years since her mom died there was nothing either. It hurt to think her aunt didn't want to reunite, but she did her best to swat those thoughts away as soon as they came. She didn't know how her aunt's health had been near the end, physically or mentally. It was possible her aunt's weathered mind had long ago forgotten her niece entirely.

Here she was walking through the door almost exactly two decades after the last time she arrived for a visit, and the scent of jasmine made her eyes well with tears. It was difficult to say what was causing the water works. Was it the missed years with an aunt she loved dearly mixed with the memories of being in the house after all this time? Was it the brutal reminder of her loss of family? Kat believed she was alone after her mom passed away, but she could've had a few more years connected, feeling like more than a shoot off the family tree that had been replanted to blossom a new lineage. Mostly she suspected it was the loss of her innocence because that's what her time in Fogpoint had always represented to her. This was the happy time of her childhood before her father's wreck when she had yet to experience pain. She returned still young by most people's means, but aged far beyond the number of birthdays she'd had with each blow life dealt her. Kat inhaled deeply and hoped the scent would never leave.

She set her suitcase down and turned around in the hallway. The house, from what she could see, looked exactly as it had the last time she was there. The side table in the hall with its basket to catch what you drop as her aunt would say. Next to it was a vase filled with a long abandoned floral bouquet. Dried petals and leaves adorned the top of the table so frail they'd crumble if she touched them. If this was any other home, she'd toss the entire vase in the trash, but this one she'd do her best to clean.

On the wall was an oval mirror with an ornate frame where her aunt would always check her reflection before leaving the house. As a child, Kat could barely see more than the top of her head in it even when standing on her tip toes. Even so, she'd find flyaway wisps of hair to tuck behind her ears and scrunch up the length in the back trying to add body, standing next to her aunt, following her lead.

The front room, or parlor as Aunt Dot called it, was filled with a mix of antiques and modern furniture. There was no television. When Kat had asked about it, her aunt would say, "A parlor is for entertaining guests. The family room is for entertaining yourself."

Kat had a feeling if she walked through the front room and opened the door to the family room, there wouldn't be a television there either. Her aunt could explain the absence of one however she wanted, but the truth was, she didn't see a need for it. She made a quick mental note, creating a to do list with buying a television and cable installation being the first items on it.

Across the hall from the front room, the pocket doors to the dining room were closed. They didn't need to be open for Kat to know what was waiting on the other side. The massive oak dining room table could seat ten. The extra leaf was always in place. "You never know who might stop by," her aunt would say.

Aunt Dot was either referencing bygone days when perhaps she did receive more company, or her visitors only arrived in the colder months. There had never been a meal when it wasn't only the two of them. It could seat ten, but there were nine chairs. The tenth one had been discovered in a bedroom upstairs while she was exploring, but she had been too young to think it odd enough to remember to ask why it was there.

Above the fireplace, there was a familial five generation painting. It had been commissioned as a ninetieth birthday present for Aunt Dot's grandmother. The grandmother was seated in the middle cradling a small infant in her arms. The other two women in the painting were her aunt's mother and daughter. Aunt Dot was the only one of the five women still alive when Kat met her. Kat's parents weren't the first tragedies to strike their families.

A buffet table lined the end wall storing, among other things, various linen tablecloths that dually served as capes for a young Kat. There was a painting above it of the cove from the viewpoint of someone on the water. The edge of the harbor was to the right, and the left side was open ocean. Whenever her aunt noticed Kat's interest in the painting, she'd tell her, "If you close one eye and squint the other while looking at those trees, you can see just a hint of my house." Kat had never been able to find her aunt's house in the painting and realized now while thinking about it how it wasn't actually there. It was something her aunt told her to keep her occupied while looking for it.

As far as art goes, it was alright. It'd never be hung in a museum or featured in a show of prominent artists. This painting along with the five generation painting were her aunt's two favorite pieces.

Aside from when she'd play as a child closing one side to create a barrier to spy behind or block off a room entirely in whatever make believe world she was playing in that day, Kat had never seen the doors closed. For a moment, she wondered if she hadn't left the doors shut on her last visit, and her aunt had never opened them again, leaving them as Kat had left them for her return.

"Don't be absurd," she muttered to herself.

Kat put her fingers into the rounded insets on the doors and tried to pull them open, but they wouldn't budge. She inspected the latches on the doors, having never realized they were capable of locking. One of the many keys in her purse would probably unlock them, but it could wait until tomorrow. At least she hoped one would because it would be a shame to have to replace or damage the doors in any way. It was her favorite features of the house how intact it was, the pocket doors throughout, original woodwork, and even push button light switches.

If she really wanted to, she could walk down the hall to the kitchen and enter the dining room through the butler's pantry. It had been partially renovated before her time to create a laundry room. One side was still the pantry, but the other had a washing machine and dryer next to the sink. She decided against it, but if she had, she would've discovered the other door to the dining room was locked as well.

It wasn't what she would typically consider to be late, but she had been driving for two days straight and was exhausted. All Kat wanted was her old bedroom, her old bed, and a good night's sleep. She picked up the suitcase she brought in with her and headed up the stairs, thinking she wouldn't even care if the bed was made. All she needed at this point was a pillow and a blanket on top of the bare mattress. Sleeping on a naked bed as her aunt called it would cause Aunt Dot to roll over in her grave. It was that final thought which guaranteed Kat would find fresh sheets in the hall closet to make the bed before she laid down.

Her bedroom was the one closest to her aunt's. She paused outside her aunt's bedroom door at the top of the stairs, but didn't dare step inside it. Down the hall was the door to her room which was locked as well. It shouldn't have come as a shock after the dining room, but it did. She fished out the key rings again and tried the keys one by one until finally finding the key which turned the tumblers in the lock. The door barely opened, leaving a space wide enough for her to step into, but she couldn't enter the room farther than the width of the door.

Kat reached along the wall for the light switch. There was too much in her way to find it. Using the flashlight from her phone, she peered into her old bedroom. It was crammed with junk. There were boxes and bags, store bags and trash bags. It looked like what started as careful stacks along the wall and on the bed had turned into a free for all. Stuff was thrown over top to land wherever it could fit. It didn't surprise her to learn Aunt

Dot had used her old room for storage except she had always been meticulous and tidy. Finding the room is such disarray was concerning.

She tried the doors of the two spare bedrooms, but those doors were locked as well. One by one, she tried all of the keys on both doors, but none of them worked. Back at her room, she wondered if she'd have the energy to make a path to the bed and then clear off the bed on top of that.

It was like her aunt's bedroom was calling to her, motioning to her, beckoning her to come to it. Kat could feel it trying to get her attention, but she ignored it. That room had always been off limits. Kat could play anywhere in the house, but she was not allowed in Aunt Dot's bedroom unless her aunt was present and invited her inside.

With a heavy sigh, she finally turned her head and looked in the direction of her aunt's old room. The hallway seemed to suddenly elongate as if her aunt's bedroom door was running away from her. It caused her to spin, and she flailed her arms out to catch her balance as the dizziness almost brought her to the floor. Then everything returned to normal. Kat blamed it on being overly fatigued.

It was settled. She would use her aunt's room just for the night. When she approached the door, she reached out with one hand, holding the keys in the other. It wasn't locked. The door swung open when she turned the knob.

The room was exactly as she remembered it. There was her aunt's four post dark mahogany bed with matching night stands adorned with antique lamps. In one corner was the desk where Aunt Dot spent most of her time journaling and writing letters. There was a full length mirror which could swivel on its base to adjust the height of the reflection it could capture or the angle.

The bed was perfectly made with the wine colored bedding set her aunt loved. Aunt Dot's dusty rose colored robe lay draped partially on the bench at the foot of the bed and partially over the mattress. Her aunt's matching slippers were on the floor in front of the bench where she left them after putting her shoes on when she prepared for the day as she called getting dressed. That's when Kat finally cried.

Chapter Three
Whack-A-Doo

IT HAD BEEN A DISCOURAGING morning already. With all the keys she had, there was none to unlock the two bedrooms upstairs or the garage. The remote for the overhead door was missing, and she couldn't budge it from the outside either. It was locked or caught on something inside, but she didn't know which. Of the thirty-nine keys, over half of them went to locks still unknown. Kat had been labeling them as she went and separating them on different keychains to organize them better.

The rooms she had managed to open were piled high as she expected after what she found in her bedroom last night. It had been quite a disappointment to see how much work lay ahead of her and how much her aunt had changed. Kat didn't know much about hoarding, but this had to be some form of it, maybe associated with old age and isolation.

All of the rooms would have to be emptied if she wanted to get a good price when she put the house on the market next year. While it was something she wanted to start tackling right away, it didn't have to be today. There were more pressing concerns like shopping for supplies first. She added economy size boxes of trash bags to her list before leaving.

There was a little delicatessan on the corner that Kat passed on her way to the grocery store. Either it sold ice cream, or it used to be an ice cream shop when she was younger. The library was a block away from that intersection, and she remembered going there with her aunt often when she'd visit. It was one of her least favorite things to do.

Aunt Dot would spend hours researching there. Kat was never sure what she was looking up or why, and she had never asked. Her aunt would turn her loose in the children's section to pick out what she wanted. The limit was five at a time. It had never been hard for Kat to find five books. If anything, it was harder to limit herself to only five. She'd bound over to the other side of the library to find her aunt, and she'd always be flipping through one book after another, jotting down notes.

It would seem like an eternity until her aunt had finished with her stack, placing them on the return cart. Kat would gather up her books again ready to go, only to have her aunt head back to the card catalogue to look up more books to pick out from the racks. In time, Kat learned to take advantage of the wait by reading to her heart's desire in the children's section until her aunt came to find her.

They'd leave the same each time, Kat with her five books and her aunt with one novel. On the walk home, they'd stop at the corner shop, and she was allowed to get any ice cream she wanted. It was her aunt's way of appeasing her after the boredom she endured at the library. She always picked chocolate in a cone or mint chocolate chip in a dish. It was still one of her many idiosyncrasies that she wouldn't eat the latter in a cone. Every time they stopped, her aunt would say, "Go on, now. Get whatever you want."

It still came as a surprise when, after years of visits, she learned she could get the triple scoop. "Whatever you want," her aunt had repeated when she asked. That was the first and last time she had one. It melted, creating the biggest, awful sticky mess, and she couldn't finish it. If that wasn't enough, the stomach ache she got from it sealed the deal.

Her aunt wouldn't pick up the book she got from the library that Kat ever noticed before going to bed, but the very next day, Aunt Dot would be ready to return to the library to do it all again. It impressed her so much as a child that her aunt was capable of reading such a long book in one night. She would wonder if Aunt Dot had even gone to sleep at all. Surely, she had to be awake all night to finish it.

As she got older, she began to challenge it, asking her aunt if she had in fact read the book, or if it was just another one she needed to look up information in it. The books her aunt brought home didn't have the same look as the ones she skimmed through at the library, but she hadn't noticed that distinction yet. Her aunt would smile and rave about the exotic places or fascinating time periods the book had helped her escape to when she unwound for bed.

On the way back from the store, she noticed how busy the little deli was as she passed which is always a good sign. Kat drove around the block to come back and find a place to park. By the time she unloaded and put away the full load of groceries she had just purchased, she'd be too hungry to want to wait to cook a meal. The inside of the shop was tiny, but the owners managed to fit several small tables inside for the lucky customers who were able to get one. The glass display on the counter presented the choices for lunch with a chalkboard menu hanging from the ceiling behind it showcasing their specials. There was a cash register near the doors, but at the far end of the counter hung a sign that read "Order Here" with a line a handful of people long.

Kat walked back and stood at the rear of the line. The people who were seated all looked up and took in a heavy glance when she went by. They were locals, regulars at this eatery, and she was a stranger. It made them take notice. If this place turned out to be as good as the line implied, she'd check to see if delivery was available in the future.

Fogpoint Harbor wasn't what you'd call a small town when she was a child, but it had grown considerably the last twenty years. It would take a while for people to learn who she was or why she was there. If it was up to her, she'd stay under the radar as long as possible. She remembered her aunt had been quite colorful and eccentric, and her presence was further proof of that.

The line moved quickly with the young man behind the counter greeting everyone by name. Two of the men in line were told to go on and head to the register because their usual was waiting on them. When it was her turn, the young man's friendly smile quickly faded. He turned professional, greeting her properly and asking how he could help her today. His eyes were filled half with curiosity and half with the standoffish nature one might expect in rural small towns when strangers came through, not the city.

"Hi," she said. "I'll take a corned beef on rye with Swiss cheese and mustard. And, um, pickle on the side, please."

He repeated her order to make sure he had it correct then asked for a name to put it under. She gave him her full first name, and he asked her to step to the side to wait.

While she waited, she wondered why she had told him Katrina. No one had called her that since she was nine years old unless she was in trouble. She had never liked the name. Truth be told, she didn't like Kat much better, but she was used to it.

The door to the deli opened, and an older man near retirement age walked in. The regulars greeted him by name, and he took a minute waving to his friends. He walked to the register, bypassing the line to checkout, and stood on the other side a foot or so away from the line instead. "What do you know, Donna?" he asked.

A young girl with a blonde ponytail yelled out a name from behind the glass display, and one of the many people waiting along the wall took their place in line at the register to pay. The girl didn't look old enough to work, but Kat figured she must be in high school.

"Not much more than I did yesterday, Harold," Donna said. The woman who was working the register smiled, but seemed annoyed by him. Her gray roots were showing on her dishwater blonde hair that was pulled up on top of her head. It was clear that she had been beautiful once, a real catch. Evidence of the stress of life and passing years was visible wherever you looked. There were a few extra pounds around her waist, and her pants struggled to keep it controlled. She probably wasn't used to being a size larger yet. The backs of her hands were no longer smooth and soft like in her youth. Wrinkles had dug deep lines in her face, and her makeup caked up in them, making them more prominent than the intended purpose of the products she used.

Harold leaned against the counter, getting as close as he could to her. It was obvious to Kat, and anyone paying attention, he was sweet on her. Sadly, Donna was sending every signal that she didn't return the sentiment. "Have you heard the news?" he asked.

"Danny!" the blonde called out. The man who had been standing next to her headed to the register.

"What news is that?" she asked. Her voice was strained, balancing between being polite while trying not to show too much interest.

"The old Libby house has a new resident," he said.

Kat's ears perked up. She felt a flush heat her cheeks, and she hoped no one else noticed it. He was talking about her, and the house that had belonged to her Aunt Dorothy Libby.

"You don't say, Harold," one of the men sitting nearby said.

Harold straightened up at the counter and looked toward the voice. "Heard it from the Chief himself down at the barbershop this morning. She arrived late last night."

How did anyone know that? Kat wondered. *Was I being watched? Or maybe someone was keeping tabs on the house?*

"Michelle! Joey!" The young girl knocked out two at once.

"She?" another man laughed. "Now, you've got my interest."

The whole deli lit up with muttering and laughter from people digesting this new bit of gossip.

"Yeah, I guess it's the old lady's niece who is taking over the house. Have you seen her?" he asked, turning back to Donna.

"Who?" The poor woman was swamped with work, and he wasn't making her job any easier.

"The old whack-a-doo's niece. Have you met her yet?" he

asked again.

Donna sighed heavily. Harold wasn't going to be easily discouraged. "Not since she was a kid," she admitted.

The old man straightened and crossed his arms clearly thinking she'd been holding out on him.

"Don't look so shocked. She used to spend every summer out here. Her name was Katrina if I remember right. Didn't care too much to be called by her full name. I learned that when I tried dropping the nickname once. That," she pointed a finger in the air for emphasis before returning to making rolls of silverware to put in the bags. "That I remember very well," she laughed. "Dot never did explain why her niece quit visiting, but she didn't explain much of nothing to anyone anyhow."

A low murmuring went through the deli. Some vaguely remembered a young girl at Dot's side during the summer months, but that was ages ago. For most of them, this was the first they learned of Dot having any living relation.

Donna glanced around the crowd. "Sweet kid from what I remember," she said just loud enough to make sure everyone heard.

"Oh!" Harold wagged his finger in the air. "You're talking about Kitty. Come to think of it I do believe I remember her tagging along with that old bat a few times."

"Kat," Donna corrected. "And be nice, Harold."

Harold shook his head and mumbled, "Kitty. Kat. Same thing."

The teenager behind the counter held up a white bag, and called out, "Katrina!"

Everyone in the deli froze in place except for their eyes which shifted to fully stare at her. Kat took the bag from the teenager and walked to the register. Harold stepped back as if 'whack-a-doo' was something you could catch.

Donna smiled at her deeply, and Kat could feel it was genuine. She wasn't having an easy time with Harold herself, so she probably could understand. "How you doing, hun?" she asked.

Kat tried to force a smile in return, but she couldn't. "Fine, thank you," she did manage to say softly.

The weight of the stares of the entire deli fell upon her back. Her movements were swift and jerky. They were all sizing her up, forming their own opinions, and judging her. The hope of blending in without attracting attention was over. Not only would the gossip spread about her being in town, but now, they'd have a recent description of her looks to add to it.

"I suppose you heard all that?" Donna asked her while ringing up her order.

"I did."

Donna read off the total. "Pay him no mind. He's nothing to do with his time now then gossip and be a bother to those who still have to earn their living."

"Bother!" Harold took offense to her choice of words.

"Don't let him get under your skin." Donna ignored the old man who was still standing far off to the side like Kat was contagious. "I hope to see you around."

Harold muttered under his breath while Donna spoke. He was rambling on about how he never bothered a soul a day in his life.

Kat paid for her sandwich and couldn't wait to leave the deli. She refused to run out. Her movements felt awkward and forced, but she took it one step at a time. Delivery it was from now on, and she'd check to see if any of the stores had a pickup option. One year was all she had to manage. After that, she'd be in the clear for life wherever she chose to live it.

Chapter Four
The Journal

KAT STOOD AT THE SCREEN door looking across the front porch at the steady drizzle of rain coming down. Her aunt's house sat on a hill that over looked the hustle of the tourist area of the town. It was conditioning that led her to call it that. Visiting here over the summer, her aunt and everyone they talked to referred to Fogpoint Harbor as a town, but the population made it much larger. There were a few other properties on the street, but this house was the last on the dead end.

The first order of business for the day really should have been to start clearing out the rooms of the house where her aunt had junk stored to see what had value, sentimental or otherwise, what could be put into a yard sale this summer, and what if anything may hold the keys to unlocking the mystery as to why her mom had told her twenty years ago that her aunt had passed away.

This spring rain changed all that. It sucked dry her momentum to start tackling any tedious jobs. Besides, this would be a slow process. Each room probably held enough for a yard sale, and there was at least a month until the season began. There was nowhere to store anything until then except to leave it in the rooms where it was currently crammed.

The rain wasn't the only thing that took her mind off the contents of the house. Her aunt had left a new journal on the bedside table with a letter sticking out of it addressed to Kat. The letter was cryptic, shrouded in riddles that she didn't understand. It was just as she remembered her aunt to be.

She went back to the bedroom that had belonged to her aunt still feeling like a little kid on the verge of getting into trouble, like she shouldn't be in there without permission. The fire she had built in the fireplace before breakfast was crackling gently and had taken the chill off the room. The journal was leather bound and thick with paper that replicated the look of long ago. She took it back upstairs to her aunt's desk and sat down, reading the letter again.

Dearest Kat,

If you're reading this, I'm sorry we didn't get a chance to say goodbye. I made a promise to your mom which even after her death, especially after her death, I vowed to keep.

I know you will find having to live here for a year is typical of your kooky old aunt. It's something unsurprising given my many quirks, but it's more than that. I want you to have the estate, Kat. You're all I have in the living world. I knew you would sell the house outright without the stipulation included in the will.

You need time to learn the house, to understand it, to realize it has more than good bones. It contains the heart as well.

Be good to the house, Kat. It will be far better to you.

Love,

Aunt Dot

Journaling was something Kat had never quite understood. It seemed dangerous writing your secrets down, putting them on the page where anyone might find them. That was essentially the main point of one. It was the first place people looked to snoop. Her aunt loved journals and would write in hers every night before bed. She had tried to get Kat interested in them, but it was to no avail. Maybe her aunt thought things had changed as she grew older, and that's why she chose a journal as a parting gift. Kat was determined to make the attempt for her aunt's sake, but she sat with pen in hand and a blank mind. There was so much she could write about her aunt, her family, and the estate, but that was a lot of ground to cover, making it hard to decide where to start.

While she thought, she stared at the hideous cat figurine on her aunt's desk. It stood about a foot tall with a rounded belly. The eyes were squeezed shut, and the front paws were clutching it's mid-section like it had ate a delicious treat. It seemed like an odd fit for the room, but her aunt had the most random items tucked away everywhere. She had probably run out of room and had to start using the bedroom for the weird junk she picked up.

A knock at the door interupted her from her thoughts. She set the pen down and noticed the page was no longer blank. It read, "Harold was murdered."

It was her handwriting, but she had no memory of writing those words. Kat jumped from her chair so fast it spun out behind her and crashed to the floor. *'Where did that come from?'* she wondered. She had only just met Harold. Sure he was a little abrasive, but she didn't wish death on anybody. She couldn't remember thinking about him while she sat there with the journal. In fact, he hadn't crossed her mind since leaving the deli yesterday. That was enough journaling for her, and she threw the leather bound book into the fireplace as she left the bedroom.

The knock came again as she reached the top of the stairs. There were a few doors in the house she couldn't find keys to including the garage and had called a locksmith that morning. There was no one else who should be coming by.

As she came down the stairs, she saw a man peering in the side window of the door. He didn't look like any locksmith she had ever seen. They didn't typically wear suits.

Kat opened the door and surveyed the man standing on her porch. He wore an old brown suit that didn't seem to fit like perhaps it once had done.

"Morning, ma'am," he said.

His word choice caused her to purse her lips. He had to be close to twice her age. 'Ma'am' was an unusual way for him to address someone so much younger.

"I'm Detective Kinley with the FHPD," he said, pulling the front flap of his suit jacket back with one hand displaying the badge he wore on his belt. It also revealed the haphazard way he tucked in only the front of his white button up shirt, leaving the rest to hang over his pants in the back. Detective Kinley tried to appear professional with his ill-fitting and sloppy manner of dress, but it made her wonder how precise and tidy the bulk of his work was handled. "Are you Kat?" he asked. "Katrina, I mean. Thompson?"

"That's right. I am," she said, opening the screen door and stepping onto the porch. She had been in town for two nights and was amused, if not a bit alarmed, as to how she managed a visit from the police department let alone a detective so soon.

A broad smile formed across his face, and he said, "It's great to see you again." He must have noticed the confused look she had because he continued. "I had met you a couple times when you were just a young'un up here visiting," he said, holding his hand out palm down a little below his waist. "You must have been no more than this high back then."

"Oh," she said. "It's been a long time."

"Nah, that's fine. I don't expect you to remember some old fart like me, but I was a friend of your aunt's."

Those were words she wasn't used to hearing. Her aunt knew many people, and they were all kind. There was only one person she ever considered to be a friend of hers, and it wasn't him.

"Anyway," Detective Kinley went on. "Some of us down at the station were just wondering if you were planning on continuing the work your aunt did for us."

"Work?" she asked. As far as Kat knew, her aunt hadn't worked a day in her life which added to the surprise of learning about the estate she left behind.

"Yeah, as a consultant with the department. She worked on a number of cases for us over the years."

"Consultant?" Kat asked, vaguely aware of her one word questions.

"You know, looking over the evidence," he began, scratching his head like he had trouble finding the words. "Giving input."

Kat understood what a consultant might do, but it was the last thing she thought she'd learn about her aunt.

Detective Kinley cleared his throat. "As you may know, the

body of Harold Murphy was discovered this morning. He had been murdered."

The hairs on the back of her neck stood straight up on end. "Harold was murdered." She repeated the words she had just seen on the page of her journal and worried why the detective suspected she was previously aware of it.

"It's already the talk of the town," the detective continued.

That would explain why he assumed she may already know about his death. At least, she hoped that was the reason.

"It's still early on in the investigation. We might not need any consultation on this one. The thing is Harold rubbed a lot of people the wrong way, but he didn't have any real enemies. Did you know him?" he asked.

Kat shook her head. "I know of a Harold, but I really don't know if it's the same Harold."

He nodded. "Met him at the sandwich shop yesterday?"

"Yes," Kat said.

"It was mentioned when we were asking around this morning. That was Harold Murphy, minding everybody's business but his own as was his nature to do. Well, alright then," Detective Kinley said. "I just wanted to introduce myself and let you know the door was open if you were considering following in your aunt's footsteps."

He peered into the house through the screen, looking down the hall. "If the house says anything to you," he began, nodding toward the door, "feel free to stop by."

"The house?" Kat asked, wishing she could do more than repeat his words as questions.

"Ah, don't mind me. It's just how I used to put things with your aunt. Hope to see you soon. Have a good day," he said and took his leave.

"Thanks. You too," she said, entirely confused by what had just happened.

Kat went inside and looked up the stairs, waiting and listening. A number of things had raised her eyebrows in the short time since she arrived. Items she'd set down would disappear only to show up hours later in an entirely different area. Doors would be open she knew she had closed and vice versa. A few strange noises left her wondering if it could be more than the house settling as she'd always heard these things being explained away.

What happened with the journal was beyond any paranormal type of activity she'd ever experienced. Kat had always been a little skeptical about ghosts and the like. There was always a logical reason to sort out anything unusual. She wanted to believe, thought it was possible, but never had the proof herself. This house made her think she may have found it.

Somewhere in her memory, there was a clip, a sound bite of spirits writing through the living. It was buried, and she couldn't pull up the file of exactly how she remembered learning it was something that was supposed to be able to occur. She thought it was only mediums who could do it, not just any random person, and she was certainly not equipped with the ability to communicate with the dead. After her dad passed away, she spent most of her adolescence attempting to contact him without any luck.

The stairs were more daunting now, almost like she was the one going to the scene of the crime instead of the detective. There was a hush in the house she had barely noticed, but the lack of noise was overwhelming her now. Each step on the stairs creaked and echoed and made her aware if there was anything in this house, she was alerting them she was coming.

Back in her aunt's bedroom, she spied the journal laying on the floor near the fireplace. She was certain she had tossed it in the flames, had the memory of seeing it consumed by the fire, but there it was, untouched and unharmed. The urge to flee came over her, but she took a deep breath and blew it out nosily with puffed cheeks. Memories can be deceiving. Maybe she saw what she wanted to see. It could've hit the side of the fireplace and bounced back as she left to answer the door.

Kat picked up the journal and inspected it. There wasn't a mark on it, not even a slight singe. For a moment, she considered throwing it back in, making sure it landed in the flames this time, but thought better of it. The journal had been a gift from her aunt, the last gift she'd ever receive from Aunt Dot. It was something she'd regret destroying.

Sitting down at the desk, she opened it to the page where the words, "Harold was murdered," had been written. It still seemed surreal the words appeared immediately before speaking with Detective Kinley. Kat picked up a pen and wrote around the existing words, changing it to say the detective stopped by telling her Harold was murdered. It made her feel a little less self-incriminating now.

Once she got started, she continued effortlessly, filling a couple pages with her shock over learning Aunt Dot worked for the police. What did she do? Why had it never been mentioned? Adding to it, she wrote about the mysteries she brought with her. Why had she been told her aunt was dead? Why had her aunt never tried to contact her? When she was finished, she felt great about getting it off her chest, having a record of her thoughts, and had a glimpse into how helpful journaling could be. Then she looked at her words.

None of her thoughts were on the pages. There were four words, one sentence, repeated across the first two pages. It read, "His grandson did it."

Kat closed the journal and ran from the room. Her instinct was to run from the house and never look back, but she left her purse with the car keys in it upstairs in the bedroom on the same desk where the journal lay. Nothing would motivate her to go into that room again so soon. Instead, she opened the dining room doors and attacked the clutter and chaos her aunt had locked inside it.

Chapter Five
Notes from the Past

THE DINING ROOM, LIKE all of the filled rooms in the house, had loomed over her, weighing her down. The task of sorting through everything her aunt had amassed since her last visit overwhelmed her. It was a project so large and tedious she couldn't find the energy to start it. Part of her wanted to hire someone, a team of people if necessary to help, but she rejected the idea. "It's a senseless use of money," she could hear her mom say. Plus, there was already too much gossip about her aunt as it was without adding hoarder to the list of the town's conversation starters.

Having a push from the unseen writer in the bedroom was more than enough to move her feet. With her car keys left in the bedroom, Kat did the next best thing. She went to work on the house. Hours passed without her realizing how long she had been working. It wasn't until pains of her hunger pointed out it was long past time to break for lunch when she stopped to assess her progress.

It was fairly organized by then with a few boxes remaining untouched. A lot of it had gone straight into the trash. There was a massive amount of mail and various other papers Kat set aside for use in the fireplaces. Most of it she couldn't understand why her aunt kept. There were thank you cards from people not specifying what her aunt had done only their gratitude for it. It was a shock her aunt knew that many people.

The only way to describe most of the items was to classify them as effeminate even though Kat understood it was wrong to do so. It was a rather equal distribution between new and old with most of the used items nearing antiquity. It resembled a collection of thoughtless gifts for adult women. Everyone seems to think all they want is something new for the home such as a toaster, candle holders, or the latest kitchen gadget. How or why her aunt amassed so much over the last twenty years was another riddle she'd probably never get answered.

There wasn't much in the room Kat really wanted to keep. It was all in good, useable condition where tossing it would be a waste. There were five more rooms like this in addition to the basement and the garage, with a few random piles in the rooms that were essentially clear. The dining room alone could account for a month's worth of garage sales, and she considered the idea of opening the doors to let people shop in the house.

'No,' she thought. *I need to go through everything.* It would give her something to do during the year she had to live here. There would be a sale every weekend this summer and a couple more next spring at the end of her stay. In fact, a year might not even be long enough to clear out the house entirely.

Kat rummaged through the kitchen, looking for something to fix for lunch. There was nothing to eat, and she had just done the shopping yesterday. *This is why you never go to the store hungry,* she thought, moving around the hodge podge mix of ready to eat and quick heat food products, hoping something else will appear on her fourth trip exploring the refrigerator and pantry.

All of this would have hit the spot yesterday when she originally planned on coming straight home to eat right away instead of cooking, but she stopped at the deli for lunch instead. The sandwich was piled high, and she could only eat half of it, saving the rest and the bag of chips for her supper. She had the time today to cook, but there was nothing to make except eggs which she already had for breakfast.

There'd be another shopping trip in the near future. This time with more planning of what meals she wanted to fix, and she would make sure to eat before leaving the house. In the meantime, she settled for microwavable macaroni and cheese cups, cooking two of them at once. When it was done, she dumped them in a bowl and drained a can of tuna to add to it. There was a breakfast nook off the kitchen, and she sat at the table moving two flat boxes of assorted junk to make room.

As she ate, she flipped through the contents of the boxes. It was mostly kindling for the fireplaces. More junk mail and thank you cards. Kat read each of them, but they were as vague as the ones from the dining room except for one. It was from a woman named Eleanor, and the handwriting gave away her age. It read, "Thank you so much for your help. It eases my mind knowing Herb is at peace. I would never have found the papers without you. I hope this check is enough."

The check was gone, but her aunt kept the card. She flipped the envelope over and looked at the postmark. It was sent August 2017, long after Kat's last visit. Most of the ones in the dining room were from the early aughts. She chuckled realizing she'd be able to tell which rooms were filled first based on the postmarks. It was an answer she hadn't even been trying to find.

She kept sorting through the boxes after she had finished her lunch wanting to finish what she started. The second box was more of the same. It was all mail, coupons, some matches and random pieces of mix matched flatware. Near the bottom, she found another card which she assumed was another note of thanks. She flipped it over to read the postmark first, June 2017.

Kat sighed seeing the date. It was the month her mom passed away. Then she noticed the city in the postmark. It was processed through Columbia. The town of Riverside where she was from was too small for the mail to be marked locally, but it went from there to Columbia. There was no return address on the envelope, and she tore the card out so hastily the envelope ripped wide open in the process.

It was a blank card with an image of a field of flowers on the front. On the inside was a hand written note signed, "Nikki Thompson." The card was from her mom, and it had to be sent around the time she died. Kat closed the card and dropped it on the table. Her heart raced like she was about to get caught snooping into something she should leave alone. She shook her head then cracked her neck. *'No, it's mine now. The house and everything in it, including the secrets.'*

She propped her elbows on the table and laced her fingers together under her chin. Ever since the lawyer told her when Aunt Dot actually passed away, she'd suspected there was continuing communication between her mom and her aunt. This was proof.

It wasn't much more than a gut feeling, but her mom had

to have known the truth. If that was the case, why wouldn't she still keep in touch with Aunt Dot? Unless they had a falling out, but Kat didn't see that being the case either. It was her dad who didn't care much for her aunt, not her mom.

The wall across from her was empty, but she stared at it, fixating on one spot to calm her nerves. There was a faint outline of a rectangle where the paint was slightly lighter than the rest of the wall. When she was a child, a painting hung there. *'Was it a painting? Or a framed picture?'* She couldn't be sure and wondered if she'd find it somewhere in the house, but she would first have to remember what had been in that spot.

With a deep breath, she picked up the card again and noticed how worn the fold was. It was separating at both ends. Her aunt had read this card numerous times. She blinked back tears from seeing her mom's handwriting and read what was written inside.

Dorothy,

I haven't been doing well for some months. The cancer came back with a vengeance. I thought I'd have more time. Don't we all? Kat doesn't know anything, and I refuse to tell her now when it may taint her memories of me. I love her more than you could ever understand. Well, maybe you do. I'm afraid this will be the last time you hear from me.

Five years. Please honor that.

Nikki

Kat read through the note several times. What had her mom not been willing to tell her? Would she ever find out the truth? Why did they agree to keep Kat from her aunt? Why was there a five year agreement of no contact after her mom's death? She put her face in her hands and wept quietly, afraid she'd never learn what it was all about and wished she could go back to her childhood when everything still made sense, and life hadn't reared its ugly head taking the people she loved away from her one by one.

'*Childhood.*' The word triggered something, and she stared at the wall again with her head tilted to the side. There had been a painting of a woman in a sundress holding the hand of a young child who couldn't have been older than the age of two. They were walking down an old dirt road with their backs turned. The left side of the road was lined with pine trees, but the right side was bordered by a barbed wire fence. There was something in the field, some out building. It had a patchwork star painted on the broad side.

The entire painting was done in muted neutral tones. It was soft and not quite real to life. The biggest splash of color were the overalls the young child wore. They were a bright vivid red, singling the child out as the focal point of the painting. It was familiar to her in a way that stood out as more than recognizing the missing painting. Something about the way she remembered the barn. The gears in her brain strained to turn, pulling a memory to the forefront of her mind, but it was unsuccessful.

Kat thought she knew the barn somehow, had seen it in person. '*No, it must just be the painting. It's putting false memories in my head.*' Now the painting was fresh in her mind, Kat remembered how much she'd always loved it. Mostly because she once owned a similar pair of overalls which made her feel like she was the child in the picture even though she was older.

It had been one of Aunt Dot's favorites too. Kat massaged

the back of her head with one hand not sure if that thought was true. It seemed like there was memory just beneath the surface of her discussing the painting with her aunt, but try as she may, she couldn't pull it up. *'It had to be,'* she decided. There had been countless paintings laying around in the dining room for her aunt to choose from. *'If it wasn't, she wouldn't have picked that one to be displayed. But, if it was, where is it now?'*

Her hair was wet and matted from sweat. Kat hadn't realized how much work she had accomplished, or rather, how much effort it had taken to complete it until she felt how sweaty her head was. Kat brought her dishes to the sink and washed them before getting back to the rest of the dining room. It was only a few boxes. She'd finish them then call it a day rewarding herself with a much deserved, and needed, shower.

The last of it was more of the same. One box was filled with newspapers in their entirety. There must be something in them causing her aunt to save a copy. The publication dates ranged over a large spread beginning in the eighties. Kat wanted to give them a better once over before adding them to the fire starter pile near the fireplace. Maybe they contained articles related to her aunt. It was unlikely. Her aunt didn't like to make waves from what she could remember. If it was important enough for her aunt to keep, it was important enough for her to try and figure out why.

The other two boxes were filled with assorted home décor and other items people accumulate here and there. A few tools Kat set aside in case that's all her aunt had. There were a few sunflower decorations she kept for herself, but the rest of it could be sold. The rest that didn't go straight into trash bags like motel soaps and free samples her aunt had received in the mail anyway. The coupons attached to those expired as far back as 1994. Kat would've been a year old then which meant her aunt had been hoarding as long as she had been alive. It was just hidden better when she was younger.

Kat made her way upstairs to relax in a hot shower making mental notes as she walked. She'd need to find a few tables and put an ad in the paper for the sale. *'Is that still how it's done?'* She wasn't sure, but it couldn't hurt. She'd get a couple signs and maybe a few balloons to put at the end of the drive and on the corner down the street. Although, she had a feeling if she listed the sale at the Libby house, everyone in Fogpoint would know where she meant.

Kinley's name popped into her head, and she closed her eyes. That was something else she needed to figure out. She wouldn't be much help to the department, but he might be able to answer some questions about her aunt. *'What questions? He wouldn't know why she hoarded.'* She understood anything he could tell her about Dorothy Libby would be appreciated. Kat was beginning to feel like she never really knew her aunt at all.

She walked into the bathroom and looked at her reflection. Bags that dark and large hadn't shown on her face since college. Kat rubbed her temples. This was enough for one day. Everything else could be figured out later.

Chapter Six

Human Resources

KAT ARRIVED AT THE police department unsure of what to expect. She parked in the visitors section of the lot and had to talk herself into going in the building. There was no appointment to keep or contact name to ask for when she arrived. It felt almost ridiculous, and she was certain the person who fielded her would have no idea why she was there.

'What am I supposed to say? I'm here to apply for my aunt's job even though I have no aptitude for this line of work.'

It took a couple attempts to psych herself up before she finally pulled herself out of her car. More than anything, she wanted to learn more about her great aunt. Maybe someone here at the station, someone who had worked with her could help her out. They already knew more than Kat; she had no clue her aunt ever worked for the police. It wasn't the biggest surprise she learned about Aunt Dot by any means.

Kat opened the door to the station. There was a long hall straight ahead. To the right was a smaller hallway with a little counter built into the wall about halfway down. It was protected by a glass barrier with only about four seats to sit in if you had to wait. They were full, and twice as many people leaned along the wall or sat on the floor.

There was a brief fight or flight instinct to run back outside. It had never occurred to her there might be people present while she asked about what Detective Kinley had told her. *'Hi. I was told to come down to see about being a consultant, but I don't know about what or how to do it.'*

Before she could chicken out, the woman behind the desk spotted her. "May I help you?" a voice called out.

Kat couldn't see the officer, but the voice came from the circular window intercom in the glass barrier. If she ran out now, it'd make her look too suspicious, and it might be enough to warrant an officer or two coming after her in the parking lot. She walked up to the window. "Hi, I'm Katrina Thompson," she said. "Detec-"

The officer beamed. "Yes, Miss Thompson. We've been expecting you. I'll buzz you through," she said, pointing to the door on the wall past the counter.

It gave her pause for a moment. That was the last thing she expected. She turned to walk to the door and noticed everyone in the tiny waiting area were staring at her. They didn't seem angry like she had jumped the line, but they were curious. It made her wonder how much of it was general inquisitiveness, or if word had got around town already about her arrival. They might be gawking at her because they recognized the name.

The buzzing sound was faint on this side of the window, and there was a loud click as the door unlocked. Kat pulled it open and went through. It was another hallway with outside exit doors at the end. She could see light shining through them, pouring into the far end of the hallway. There was a glare, so all she could see was a blinding white light except for a small potted plant in the corner on the other side of the doors.

On her left, a door opened, and the woman who buzzed her in popped her head into the hallway. "About halfway down, take the hallway on the right. Second door on the left. I'll let her know you're on your way." She closed the door and vanished as quickly as she appeared.

'Her,' Kat thought. *'Who's her? I thought I was meeting with Detective Kinley.'*

In less than two minutes, she was standing outside the office she had been directed to. The brass plate on the door read, "Angela Watts, HR". Kat gave the door a soft knock, and a voice replied, "It's open."

She peeked her head inside slowly. It was a small office, and the woman behind the desk wasn't wearing a uniform. Kat wasn't sure why she expected her to be in the familiar blue clothing and was surprised to see her dressed in a black pant suit instead. Ms. Watts sat behind the desk with her hair pulled up in a messy bun, pen in her mouth, and both hands flying across her keyboard. There were a pair of glasses resting on top of her head.

"Av ah eet," Ms. Watts said, talking around the pen in her mouth.

Kat sat in one of the chairs on the side of the desk closest to her, taking the one nearest to the door. It was an exit plan habit brought on by her nerves.

Ms. Watts held up one finger indicating it would only take a minute. Kat looked around the room. One wall was a typical office showcase with bookshelves on the top two thirds and cabinets on the bottom. It was filled with books and binders.

There were a couple small plants and a painting on the wall of a bicycle. It was a little bare relatively speaking. The biggest stand out was the lack of photo frames. There wasn't a single personal picture in the office which she wondered if it had anything to do with safety reasons.

"Alright," Ms. Watts said, turning away from the computer with her pen no longer between her teeth. She stood up and extended her free hand, "Katrina Thompson, correct?"

Kat stood and shook her hand. "Yes, but I go by Kat."

Ms. Watts nodded. "I'm Angela Watts, head of HR here at FHPD. Let's get started."

They sat down, and Ms. Watts pulled a small stack of papers from the side of her desk and began doling them out to Kat. It was standard new hire paperwork like tax forms, employee handbook, insurance information, and so on. "Did you bring your two forms of ID with you?" she asked.

This was moving along fast, and Kat wasn't sure what to do. "Um, I have it, but I don't know what I'm doing here."

"You're a new hire, right?" Ms. Watts checked something in the computer. "Consultant for the department?"

Kat's throat tightened, and her mouth felt dry. "It was mentioned to me as a possibility, but I don't know what I'd do for them. I'm not sure I can help."

Ms. Watts pursed her lips together and drummed the desk with her fingertips. "I see," she muttered. "One minute," she said, picking up the phone and dialing an extension.

"Hey," she said, smiling like she was talking to an old friend. "It's Watts."

"Uh-huh. I have Katrina Thompson in my office."

"Yeah, um... What exactly did you tell her about the

consulting position her aunt had with us?"

"Yeah."

"Huh."

"Well, no, she hasn't been informed of anything I don't think."

"Okay. That sounds great." Ms. Watts cradled the phone and sighed. "This is what I would like to do. Since you're already here, let's get through some of this paperwork. I'll hold off on the background checks and won't file any of this until after you talk to Kinley. He's in his office at the jail now. You'd have to go over there for fingerprinting anyway."

Kat eyed the papers on the desk. Talking to Detective Kinley was a must, but she wasn't sure about the rest of it.

"It looks like you're thinking awfully hard over there," Ms. Watts said.

"I'm worried this might be a waste of time," Kat said.

Ms. Watts shrugged. "If it is, it won't be the worst thing that's happened to me on the job. Besides, Kinley doesn't think it is."

"Fine," Kat agreed. She signed her name to at least a dozen documents and handed her ID to Ms. Watts to copy. When she was finished, Ms. Watts instructed her where to go inside the police station at the county jail and pointed out she'd have to come back to watch orientation videos before she could be put on the payroll.

Kat made her way back to her car trying to figure out what building this was if not the police station. It must be other offices that don't do field work of any kind, but it's what came up when she searched for an address to plug into her GPS. The actual police station was only a few blocks away.

Knowing Detective Kinley was expecting her didn't stop her from considering going home instead. If anything, it made the urge stronger, but she fought it.

At the police station, Detective Kinley was waiting near the main doors for her. He was laughing with a few officers when she walked inside, but he saw her immediately and waved, excusing himself from his colleagues to head in her direction. "Miss Thompson!" he said. "Happy to see you again."

The corners of her mouth pulled up in a miserable attempt to smile and probably made her look as awkward as she felt. "Thanks," she said quietly. "You too."

He led her to the elevator, and they went down one floor. "So Katrina," he said. "It's Katrina, right? Or do you prefer Kat?"

"I don't prefer either of them, but Kat is the better of the two," she said.

Detective Kinley smiled at her for a moment then laughed. "Well, okay then. Kat it is."

The elevator doors opened, and she followed him down the hallway. She was taken back to the day she met him on the front porch, and the thoughts she had about his office. Her imagination hadn't been far off the reality.

His desk was a cluttered mess. He was probably one of those people who claimed to have a method to their madness. If someone organized his office, he probably wouldn't be able to find anything again. Meanwhile, there wasn't a clear available surface anywhere except for his desk chair.

There were books stacked up on top of a couple boxes near one wall. He had a couch along another wall, and there were various suit jackets laying over one arm with boxes piled on the cushions. The couch was next to another door, and she was curious if his office had a bathroom. He could practically live here if it did, and it almost looked that way.

"Let me get that for you," he said, clearing a pile of books, mail and a takeout container off one of the chairs across from his desk and balancing it on the boxes on the couch. "There," he said, smiling and motioning for her to sit down.

Kat took a seat, but kept to the edge. Truth was she'd rather stand, but didn't want to be rude.

Detective Kinley sat on the other side of his desk and tried to fold his hands on top of it, but there was too much clutter in his way. He piled it up and placed it on another stack on the side of his desk, but the wayward tower proved to be too much. The top papers slid to the floor, and before he could move to stop the rest of it, half of the heap had fallen. He peered over at it and waved his hand. "It's fine. I'll get to it," he said. "So, Ms. Watts said you had some questions?"

"Yeah," Kat said.

"What about?" he asked, finally folding his arms on the desk.

Kat didn't know where to begin. "About everything," she said. "I have no idea what I'm doing here except I was offered a position I'm not sure I'm qualified to take."

Detective Kinley narrowed his eyes and clicked his tongue. "What do you know about the work your aunt did for us?"

Kat chuckled nervously and shook her head. "I didn't know she worked for the police until you told me the day you stopped by."

"I see," he said, leaning back. "How's the house?" he asked.

It was making her frustrated. *'Why will no one give me a straight answer?'* she thought. "It's a house," she replied in defeat, wishing she'd never left it to come here. There was a lot of work to do, and the house was going to keep her busy enough for the year without adding anything else to her calendar. She stared at the floor and plucked a piece of fuzz off her slacks.

"Anything unusual happen there since you arrived?" he asked.

Kat's head snapped up, and she looked at him with widened eyes. *'How does he know?'* she wondered.

"I expected as much," he said. His eyes twinkled, hinting at some inside information yet to be shared with her.

"How's that?" Kat asked, growing tired of the games.

Detective Kinley didn't answer her directly, not at first. He explained they kept her aunt on the payroll as a consultant for lack of a better way of classifying her position. They may go weeks without needing her assistance only to have her work long hours for days in a row. It varied, and it would with Kat as well.

The detective said her aunt always helped with the cases when they didn't know where to begin, when there were no leads, nothing to point them in the direction they needed to go. Sometimes she would contact them first, but if they came to her she was always more than willing to help. Rumor had it she always had been advising on cases even before they officially brought her in as an employee, and her mom had helped too before Dot. There was no record of it to prove the claim. The first record of her aunt helping to solve a case was around forty years ago, about the time she moved into the house after her own mother passed away.

There was something about the way he said house, an emphasis implying he knew more than he was letting on, understood more than Kat did about the weird occurrences in the old Victorian home. So many questions swirled in her thoughts. It seemed fairly simple what was going on at the Libby house, but she wanted to hear someone else say it, to prove she wasn't crazy. The problem was she couldn't ask the one question dancing at the forefront of her mind, couldn't put it into words where she wouldn't sound like a mad woman.

"It's more than a house," Detective Kinley stated.

Kat cocked her head to the side. She both understood what he meant and wanted it explained to her at the same time. She would soon regret hoping for the latter.

"There's…" Kinley's voice trailed off, and he looked to the side trying to find the right words. "There's someone, or something, in the house with you, isn't there? You've sensed it?"

"Something," Kat repeated quietly.

Kinley nodded slowly then let out a loud sigh. "It's haunted."

Chapter Seven
Specks

"HERE'S WHAT WE KNOW," Kinley said, kicking the door to an interrogation room shut with his foot. He set an evidence box on the table and began pulling files out of it.

There was a handful of other items in the box too in clear plastic bags with writing on it she couldn't make out, but she gathered what it was. Items collected from the scene and stored with a chain of custody attached to it. If any of those bags were opened, the case could be ruined. She stared at them wondering how, after decades of technological progress, a plastic baggie was still the ultimate tool in the storage of detective work. He motioned to a chair, and Kat pulled it back, sitting on the edge.

It made her uncomfortable being in an interrogation room, and she wanted to be ready to run at a moment's notice. Something about the cold gray brick walls and mirror on the side of the room which she knew from television allowed anyone to spy on their conversation secretly filled her with unease. There had to be a different room somewhere else in the building they could have used, even Kinley's office would be better than this.

Detective Kinley sensed her agitation. "I assure you it's just a room at present, only to give us privacy." He flashed her a one sided smile and nodded in what she guessed was an attempt at being friendly, but it came across awkward and clumsy.

It also didn't explain why they couldn't look over the evidence somewhere else. There must be some rule of protocol preventing going through the files in his office, but she wasn't sure.

"The conference rooms are full," he said, rolling his eyes up and tilting his head from side to side in thought. "Full of trash," he smiled more freely. "My office is cluttered, but the conference rooms need a deep haz-mat cleaning."

Kat laughed and felt the tension slowly melt away. That remark did the trick to ease her nerves. If it was worse than Kinley's office, she was thankful to have an alternate to use even if it was this small dreary space.

"Tell you what," he said, standing and walking across the room. He reached behind the camera in the corner near the ceiling and felt around for something.

She couldn't see what he was doing, but the red light on the front of the camera went off. Her eyes narrowed, and she wondered if he turned it off or on.

"There," he said, returning to his seat. "The red light meant it wasn't recording, but now it's unplugged. You don't have to worry about someone turning it on accidentally or out of curiosity." He smiled at her and gave her a quick nod.

Kat took a deep breath and nodded back. She was as ready as she was going to get. Crime scenes were something she was only familiar with in the documentaries she sometimes streamed. It had always fascinated her how detectives could take the smallest fragments and track down the culprit. The forensics and psychological profiling astounded her like magic tricks to a child. There was a secret to it even if she didn't quite understand how it was done. Being faced with the evidence in person was something she wasn't certain she could handle, but time would very soon tell on that.

Detective Kinley pulled a couple files from the box and went through them. "Here we go," he said. "Harold Murphy."

He half tossed a picture on the table, and it slid toward her. Kat almost didn't recognize the man from the café in the photo. He looked softer, almost kind, and he was smiling. The man she encountered on her first full day back in Fogpoint didn't come off as someone capable of displaying such a warm emotion. It was a side of Harold she would've never met regardless of how long he might have lived if not for what happened. During their brief interaction, he didn't seem like he was someone who would've ever given her a chance because of who her aunt happened to be.

"Harold Murphy," Kinley began. "Sixty-seven years old, retired, and aside from being a royal pain in the butt, very well liked in town."

Kat raised an eyebrow at his choice of description.

Kinley laughed. "Don't get me wrong. He rubs people the wrong way, but that was just how Harold was. He didn't have enemies."

She nodded slowly, eyeing the folders he was holding. There was far worse to come, and she jumped between holding her breath and taking deep breaths while not wanting the detective to see how nervous she was. "Detective Kinley," she said, hoping to get this rolling.

"Frank," he interrupted. "Call me Frank. We're colleagues now."

The corner of her mouth turned up. He looked like a Frank. He was friendly and pleasant while also messy and disorganized. It was every Frank she'd ever met. "Frank," she said, "what happened to him?"

He looked at her for a moment, considering how to proceed then nodded. "He was found at the base of the stairs," he said, opening one of the files and laying it open on the table.

Kat could see most of the pictures as he shuffled through them. Most were close-ups of small specific pieces of evidence, but the pictures of Harold's lifeless body were there too.

Frank slid one across the table to her, and she couldn't take her eyes off it. He didn't say anything for a couple minutes, and she was thankful because she wouldn't have been able to follow his words. When he did speak, he was a couple sentences in to what he had to say before her mind processed there was another person in the room with her again.

"He fell?" she asked, unsure of exactly what Frank had been saying. It didn't look like a murder unless he had been pushed, but if they could prove that, they'd already have a suspect.

The detective cocked his head to the side, assessing how well she was listening if at all. "No, but it appears as though he did." He opened his mouth wide, drawing in a deep breath. "There's more to it than that."

He pulled a picture from the second file. "Are you sure you're okay to go on with this?" he asked.

Kat nodded, but Kinley was staring at her, waiting for more. "Yes," she said. Taking a deep breath, she resolved herself and looked him in the eye. "I'm ready."

THE PICTURE KINLEY showed her stuck in her mind the rest of the day. As Kat lay in bed that night, she kept seeing Harold's lifeless body laying at the bottom of the stairs. The darkened patch of carpet around his head wasn't from poor lighting. It was from the blood which spilled out of the wound on his head.

According to Kinley, Harold was knocked unconscious, but he hadn't died immediately. If it had been an accident, he could very well still be alive had someone called an ambulance sooner. As it was, he was still alive when the paramedics arrived the next morning. His pulse was weak, and he was rushed to the hospital where they were prepared to do everything in their power to save him. They never got the chance. He passed before he made it to the operating room. If he had survived, he likely wouldn't have been the same after the attack due to the amount of swelling on the brain and the time elapsed before

1. http://www.clker.com/cliparts/7/6/9/b/13309573511112670181decorative-lines-2_large-md.png

receiving treatment. Still, he may have had enough wits about him to identify his attacker.

Whoever attacked Harold might not have known he was still alive. Kinley hadn't been able to answer the question with certainty. There was no evidence on the body anyone had checked him over, but that also didn't entirely rule it out either. Kinley figured the attacker either intended to kill him and thought he'd been successful, or he didn't mean to do it and ran. The latter was just as bad if not worse in Kat's opinion. Accidents happen, even tragic ones. To leave someone to die slowly and alone to avoid getting caught was unforgivable in her mind.

It made her wonder about her aunt. She had been found in her bed the morning after she passed away. Apparently, she had phoned someone the night before asking to be checked on in the morning. If not for that, her aunt could've laid there for days before anyone noticed the town's crazy lady hadn't been around seen recently. It was like her aunt knew what was going to happen, but what Kat didn't know was how. It could've just been a feeling. There was nothing to indicate it was the first time her aunt requested a morning check either.

Kat rolled over trying to get comfortable for the seventh time since lying down. She had never looked closely at the death certificate to see what was listed as the cause of death, and now she was afraid to find out. All the lawyer said was her aunt had died in her sleep and mentioned old age. Kat took those words at face value. Aunt Dot was already old at the time Kat believed she had originally passed away. To live another twenty years on top of that was a blessing, and old age was an acceptable cause.

"I wonder if there were signs." Kat said to the empty room as she sat up. If her aunt had reason to suspect something might happen, there had to be clues. "A heart attack would wake you up, wouldn't it?" It worried her now whether her aunt passed peacefully, or if she had woken in the night in pain and alone, left to suffer by herself until the mercy of death took her.

"No," Kat said sternly. She turned the bedside lamp on and got out of bed, slipping on her aunt's robe and slippers like she had every morning since arriving. It was an homage at first, but was quickly becoming habit. "There's no point in thinking that way."

If her aunt had woke up from whatever it was that took her life, she could've called for help. That's what Kat chose to believe, and she knocked any alternate ideas out of her head as soon as they piped up their opinion. "But why didn't she go to be checked out the night before if she wasn't feeling well?" She asked the empty room another question she didn't expect to be answered, but it was.

It was sitting on the desk across the room underneath the insanely ugly ceramic cat positioned like it was guarding the journal. Kat walked over and sat in her aunt's old chair, playing with the cover by flipping it open and shut between her finger and thumb. *'Of course she had warning.'*

The journal had warned her aunt. *'Not the journal.'* Whatever controlled the journal told her what she needed to know. *'But why didn't she call?'* A cry caught in Kat's throat, and her shoulders slumped. Regardless of any deal Aunt Dot made with her mother, she could've called her one last time, especially if she knew her end was near.

"There's one way to find out." Kat slammed the cover back

and flipped to a blank page. She picked up a pen and positioned her hand over it and waited, but nothing happened. This was new to her, and she had no idea how it worked. "Aunt Dot, are you here?" She asked the question to the room, but felt uncomfortable with the cat's eyes fixed on her.

Kat turned the ceramic figurine to face the wall. If it wasn't for her aunt, she would've already tossed it in a box to be sold not that she thought there was hope of anyone actually wanting to buy it. Her aunt loved it enough to keep it on her desk, so Kat would too. It was going back home with her though. She would get rid of it by the time she left Fogpoint. She picked up the pen and waited. Her hand never moved. No words appeared on the page. She tried again. "Do you have a message from my aunt?"

It might be skipping a step. Whoever, more like whatever, was writing in the journal through her hand was unknown to her. It could be her subconscious acting out from the stress of the last few months. If a therapist was handy, she was certain it's what she'd be told. Automatic writing, as she discovered it was called during a quick internet search, isn't real. "Ugh," she groaned, tilting her head back. The point was she had no idea what spirits were in this house if that's what they even actually were. Kat had never believed in ghosts, not seriously, and she wasn't sure she was ready to start now.

That was something she could actually find an answer to herself. She could start with the library and look up the history of the house. Spirits usually stick around when something traumatic happened to them. She couldn't remember where she heard that, but it was probably on some show she watched late at night when she couldn't find anything else that looked good. There could be something in the past on this property if not the house itself.

'Seriously? This is what you've become.' If she wasn't careful, she would soon live up to the whack-a-doo family name.

When she looked back at the journal, to both her surprise and relief, she saw three words had indeed been written. It was a short lived reprieve because once again, it only created more questions instead of providing any answers. It certainly didn't give any information for the one she had just presented to the room.

"Find the specs."

'The what?' Kat sighed and leaned back, dropping the pen. She rubbed her forehead with her fingertips wondering if she was to search for a pair of glasses or a detailed set of instructions for building. Then she looked again and realized she had misread it.

"Find the specks."

Kat stood up and walked back to the bed. "Specks of what?" She pulled the blanket back, turned off the lamp and laid down. "Specks of normalcy?" Once she was comfortable she gripped the blanket under her chin. "Specks of my old life?" Kat closed her eyes and drifted off to sleep almost immediately.

Chapter Eight
Crime Scene

DETECTIVE KINLEY PICKED her up at nine sharp. For as messy and unorganized as he was, punctuality was surprisingly one of his strong points. "Are you sure you want to do this?" he asked, escorting her to the unmarked Sedan.

If anything, Kat was positive she absolutely did not want to join him at Harold Murphy's house this morning. The crime scene would be relatively clear by now. Harold's body had long been removed. It would've been photographed from every angle and evidence enough for three storage boxes collected. There wasn't anything at the scene that filled her with apprehension. She wasn't one to get faint at the sight of blood. Morbid details never turned her stomach.

Simply put, she felt like a fraud. There was nothing on her resume to even hint she would be qualified for this position. It was offered to her on the basis of who her aunt was, more specifically because she lived in her aunt's house. There was something about the old Victorian home everyone seemed to understand but her. It was something she was only beginning to figure out. It was like an inside joke that didn't include her.

Part of her wanted someone to come out with it and tell her the truth. Part of her worried if what she was starting to suspect was true, she wouldn't make it to the end of the week without fleeing Fogpoint, much less the rest of the year.

It wasn't until Kinley brought the car to a stop in front of a house in a residential neighborhood when Kat became aware he was talking and probably had been the entire drive. She hadn't heard a word he said and hoped he hadn't gone over anything important pertaining to what to do once inside the house.

"Try not to be nervous," he said. "There are no expectations. There were many cases where your aunt had nothing to offer us." He got out of the car letting his words trail back to her.

Kat stepped out on the driveway and stared at the house. It was a modest, unassuming home. She looked at the other houses on the street. They were all similar in size and value. It seemed like a good quiet place to live. It was the type of neighborhood where you'd want to raise a family. The neighbors were probably terrified now over the idea of a murder so close to home. They would be triple checking their locks at night, possibly installing security cameras around the house, and tightening the reigns on their children at least for a while.

"No one's home, but they're expecting my visit. When you're ready to head on inside... Take your time," Kinley said from the front step.

When she neared him, he unlocked the door and pushed it open. He led her to the base of the stairs. A large section of the carpet had been removed. From her experience watching forensic shows, she figured it had been covered in blood. The wood and padding peeking out where the carpet had been were covered in dark stains.

He was reciting information memorized from the case notes. "Murphy was discovered here." Kinley used his hands to give a rough impression of where the body lay. He continued, "Just after eight in the morning by his maid."

"Maid?" Kat was surprised. She didn't have Harold pegged as someone who could afford hired help.

"Cassie Evans came by twice a week to help with a few things he couldn't quite take care of anymore," Kinley explained. "Bad knees."

Kat nodded and smiled, encouraging him to continue.

"She let herself in with her key and saw the body lying in a pool of blood. She didn't touch the body because it appeared to her that he was dead and called 911 immediately."

"Was anything stolen?" Kat asked.

"No," Kinley said quickly. "Nothing was noticed missing right away. We asked his daughter to let us know when she had a chance to go through the house, but she hasn't discovered anything yet."

Kinley walked up the stairs with Kat at his heels. "And you're sure he didn't just fall?" As soon as the words were out, she remembered how he told her on the porch the day they met that Harold had been murdered. It was mentioned at the police station how they came to the conclusion of foul play. She couldn't remember the details. Everything had been overshadowed by the pictures of Harold's lifeless body.

He stopped halfway up. "It was definitely a possibility in the beginning, but the kids in the lab ruled it out. They crunched the numbers and did the math using trajectories of the head wound, angle of the body and blood splatter. Nothing lines up with an accidental fall to land him in that position."

While she didn't expect to see anyone dusting for prints or collecting hairs out of the carpet, but she assumed the home would still show a few remnants of having been a crime scene. She imagined the yellow tape would be left hanging in a few various places, and some of the plastic evidence markers might still be in place. There was nothing of that nature left, nothing to indicate an untimely death had occurred here. It made her feel even more uncomfortable. She was no longer assisting a detective at the scene of a murder; she was an intruder in someone's home.

At the top of the stairs, Kat noticed the stair post was missing the decorative finial that would've matched the one on the other railing. The other one was gone too. She ran her fingers along the top of the post underneath where it would've sat. The wood was a lighter shade having not been stained to match.

Detective Kinley eyed her as she played with the area where the finial was missing. When she caught him watching her, her breath raked over her teeth as it clicked. "The murder weapon?" she asked.

He nodded and touched the one across from her. "We're waiting to see if the other one matches the injuries on his skull, but I believe it is. And, it's missing."

Kat snatched her hand off the top of the stairs. Suddenly, it didn't feel right touching and examining the shades of the wood anymore.

"That one," he said, nodding toward Kat, "had been loose

for quite some time. The maid couldn't be sure how long, but it sat down in there and could be picked up easily. Harold hadn't been in a big hurry to have it fixed."

She listened as he continued, but his words seemed to come from farther away and echoed back to her ears. A flush swept over her cheeks, and her body temperature rose several degrees. If the room began to spin, she'd have no choice than to reach out for the railing, and she hoped it didn't come to that. She was going to have a hard time touching any stair rail again after today.

Kinley was explaining the head wound. Harold had been struck from behind on the left side of the skull. The blood splatter indicates the attacker made a full swing with whatever object was used. He demonstrated by lifting his hand in the air and striking it forward hard as if to hit something, but his hand continued downward until it finally stopped just past Kinley's hip behind him. There were little droplets of blood all around them which Kat hadn't noticed until Kinley pointed them out to her. They were on the stairs, the hard wood of the hallway flooring and some along the lower half of the wall.

They believe Harold fell forward, either from the force of the hit or from losing his balance, and tumbled down the stairs until he came to a stop on the floor near the bottom. At that point, the attacker fled, avoiding Harold's body and the pool of blood forming under his head. There was nothing tracked outside the house.

Kat stared at the dried drops of blood Kinley showed her. She followed them from the far rail on the stairs to the wall and back again. While she still didn't understand how she could provide any insight into this case, she wanted to be here, to be a part of it. She worried if he noticed how she was reacting to the scene and the details he was providing, he'd call the whole thing off. He'd take her back home and never involve her again. That meant she had to keep her head down, so he couldn't see anything.

"Murphy knew his attacker," Kinley was saying. The rest of his words droned together while Kat maintained her focus on the blood. It was something about how Harold either let the person into his home, or the attacker had access to keys and alarm codes for the house.

"And you said no enemies?" Kat asked, more to prove she was following the conversation than anything.

"That's right. Other than being mildly irritating, he was a pretty decent guy."

Kinley stared down the stairs to the floor below. "We went through the usual suspects. His family checks out. They had alibis, and none of them had motive. No one was cut from the will or anything." Kinley looked at her with a smile and a wink. "We checked into his former business partners. All good. He didn't owe anyone money." Kinley shrugged and shook his head.

"It doesn't make sense." Kat tilted her head looking at the wall.

"You got that right. It lines up to be a random attack, a robbery, but there's no evidence of it."

Kat glanced at the detective not sure what he was talking about at first. It took a minute for her mind to catch up to the last several things he said.

"You were talking about the attack?" Kinley saw her confusion.

She turned back to the wall, but didn't say anything.

"See something?" His voice moved closer to her.

The short answer was yes, but she was afraid of being wrong.

"What is it?" he asked.

Kat opened her mouth to speak, but stopped herself.

"Go on."

He wasn't going to let it drop. "It just looks like something was there," she said, motioning to an area at the top of the stairs near the floor."

Kinley didn't say anything, but he watched her, waiting for her to continue.

"These little spots of blood, where they are. I don't know. Why isn't there anything here?" She outlined the area with her finger.

"Something was in the way," Kinley agreed.

"But what? If it was a person, it wouldn't be so..." She couldn't find the word to finish her thought.

"Wide? Short? Boxy?"

"Exactly," she said relieved. At least Kinley was acting like it made sense.

"Very good. It's the last piece I haven't filled you in on yet."

Kat smiled and felt good about having figured something out on her own. It didn't help solve the case, but it did make her feel a little less useless.

"Our forensics agree something was sitting here when the attack occurred. It prevented the blood splatter from covering the wall, and it's..." He pulled out his notebook to check something. "Whatever was there measured around forty by thirty."

"You don't know what it was?"

"Nope," he said, tucking the notebook back in his pocket. "Whatever it was, the attacker took it with him."

'Then something has to be missing.' Kat kept the thought to herself because she was fairly confident someone at the department would've already considered that.

Not much was said during the drive home, but Kinley's last words to her before leaving Harold's house kept replaying in her mind. "Take your time. Wait for the house to talk to you if it has something to say."

It was her aunt's house, her house the detective was referring to, but it didn't make sense. That wasn't entirely the truth. Things were starting to add up. It was the math which didn't follow standard rules. Two and two can't possibly equal five regardless of how much anyone tried to convince her otherwise.

Ghosts weren't real. There was no such thing as transparent forms that roamed the halls of old buildings frightening the owners. It was light, exhaustion, and stress playing tricks on the mind. Orbs were specks of dust caught in the frame of a picture. The noises and things going bump in the night were nothing more than the groans of an old home settling or an overactive imagination. There was a logical explanation for everything.

Imprints could be left behind. She did believe some people could pick up on those remaining traces of energy better than others. She was not one of those people. Never had been and never would be.

The few things she'd experienced in her aunt's house since arriving like the writing in the journal couldn't be explained at least not by her. It did seem too heavy a coincidence for it to be simply that. Whatever caused her to write the words in the journal was something she wanted to figure out and was terrified to learn at the same time, but she was positive the explanation would be rooted in the real world, not in supernatural make believe.

'Or would it?' Each of these experiences coupled with others' nonchalant attitude toward their obvious belief in an other worldly hand at work in the Victorian house had her questioning herself. If there was some spirit behind it, she wasn't sure how she'd react. Everything she built her belief systems around would be destroyed.

When she stepped out of Kinley's car, she looked at the house, staring at the windows of the top floor and wondered if anything was trapped on the inside watching her arrive. Kat still held firm it wasn't more than superstition and new age hocus pocus, but she could feel her foundation begin to crack. There had to be someone, someone other than Kinley, who held some insight about the house or the property. All she had to do was find the right person, but she didn't know where to begin to look.

'So ghosts might be real.' She laughed quietly as she walked across the porch. Honestly, it shouldn't be a big surprise considering everything else she had learned the last few weeks. Nothing had been quite as she always thought it to be. *'Ghosts.'* She opened the front door and walked into the house.

Kat inhaled heavily and set her purse on the table in the hall. "Well," she said, spinning around, "talk to me."

Chapter Nine
Priced to Sell

KAT'S FIRST AND LAST garage sale had customers parked along the street, waiting in their cars when she began carrying out totes, boxes, bags, and various other armfuls of items from the dining room to display a full thirty minutes before her advertised start time of 8 am. It ended with a sell out four hours later. The journey from point A to point B, however, was filled with sharp curves, bumps in the road, and not one, but two phone calls to the police. The questions around how her aunt had amassed so much junk over the years as well as why she stowed it all away instead of unburdening herself from it were answered during the ordeal.

There was a curiosity in town revolving around her aunt. It was something she had noticed as a child the last time she had come for a visit. She had only just arrived at the age where she had begun to notice how others treated her. Everywhere she went with her aunt there were just as many people who would stare as there were people who couldn't look directly at them.

Friends would huddle together, pointing and whispering, then look away whenever Kat noticed them. Aunt Dot waved her concerns away when she mentioned them, saying, "You know how small towns are. People talk."

Except Fogpoint wasn't exactly a small town. Kat was from a small town, population 3800, according to the signs posted on the roads leading in and out. Fogpoint Harbor was the biggest city she had ever seen at the age of nine.

It wasn't something she dwelled on when she returned home. The memories had faded, and some were almost forgotten by the time she came back. In the few short weeks since her return, everything was coming back to her with vivid force as the focal point of the town's gossip shifted from her aunt to herself.

Because of this, she expected the sale to have a good turnout. People would arrive out of sheer nosiness for lack of anything else. They would be intrigued to meet Kat and see who this woman was that had inherited the Libby house for themselves. There would also be a natural curiosity to see what the belongings that once adorned the interior of the home they had never been allowed to view.

Whether they arrived to simply gawk or make a purchase wasn't as easy to assume, but there had been a lot of valuable items in that room. Some of it Kat would have bought herself in a garage sale back home, but there was simply too much of it to keep. Absolutely no one has a need for fourteen near identical working sewing machines.

Everything was priced to sell. It wasn't about making a profit so much as it was to clean it out. She hoped even those who came to feed their fascination might spy something they'd enjoy at a price they couldn't refuse.

Kat had parked her car on the street last night and could

fill the entire driveway easily enough, but there was only the two long folding tables she had spotted in the basement while standing on the fourth step from the bottom. It was as far as she could go without having to move anything out of her away. Clearing a path barely wide enough for her to pull the tables to the stairs where she could drag them up and give them a good cleaning had taken two hours. Most of the progress had been hindered by tall stacks and piles falling over as she made her way through. Most of the stuff she brought outside would have to remain in the totes and the boxes for people to dig through.

A few people didn't wait for her to finish setting up. They left their vehicles and started a slow approach up the driveway while Kat made her second trip in the house. It made her uneasy to leave everything outside with no one she knew well enough to trust watching over it. She didn't want to think someone would grab what they wanted while she was inside, but people steal packages off of porches in broad daylight. The world was a stranger now compared to its former self.

In hindsight, the smart move might have been to clear out the garage first. It would be easier to set up the night before then all she would have to do is open the automatic garage door to begin instead of having people stand around watching her get ready. If a spring shower unexpectedly sprung up as they often do, all she would have to do is close the door as opposed to rushing to get everything back inside before it was ruined.

The tables were leaning against the garage. When she headed in that direction, two men ran up, offering to help. One was from the original group who had been waiting on her after her first trip outside, and the other had just joined the continuously growing crowd. They carried the tables over and set them up near where she had lined up everything she carried from the house.

It was almost unnecessary. The moment she began lifting lids on the totes people gathered around, sorting through what was inside of them. Kat had made over a hundred dollars before she opened all the boxes and almost triple that before she finally had a chance to put anything on the tables.

The first hour of the sale had gone well, exceeding all of her expectations. Although it did raise a few curiosities of her own. A few of the people had been looking for something specific. The middle aged stout woman who had been one of the first customers of the day didn't merely ask if Kat had any fine China for sale. She inquired about a specific vintage rose design made by Homer Laughlin in the 1940's while clutching her purse so tightly she rolled the top of it over, and Kat could see the strain in her knuckles. There was an older gentlemen with an odd part in his hair that made Kat wonder if it was natural or a toupee. He wasn't looking for just any cuckoo clock, but a black forest clock with two dancers made by Helmut Klammerer.

The first specific request Kat chalked up to wishful thinking, but by the time the third one was made, she started to wonder if this was how people did things on the east coast. It wasn't until the last specific request made by Ida Rothstein when it clicked. It dawned on Kat that if she could somehow manage to fit the entirety of what her aunt had amassed over the years outside at one time, everyone would walk away with what they had been hoping to find.

Ida was an older woman, but her features gave away she was younger than her snow-white hair might make you believe.

She was looking for an antique silver flatware set stored in a box with red lining. Kat cut her off before she listed the details about the manufacturer because it wasn't necessary. There might be a set of silver somewhere in the house. If there was, it might be something she'd consider keeping for herself to be honest. There hadn't been any in the dining room where one would expect to find it. Kat informed Ida there was no silver for sale.

"Don't lie to me!" the stout woman yelled at her.

It caught Kat off guard, and she glanced around at the dozen or so other customers who had turned their heads at Ida's response as if she was trying to find the adult child to come claim their mother. "I'm not lying," she began to explain.

"This set is in that house. I know it is!" she insisted.

Kat wondered what she meant by that and figured the woman must've been over to see her aunt at some time and saw it while she was there. "That may be true," she said, "but I didn't come across anything like that in what I've gone through so far."

"May be true," Ida snickered. "Your aunt was a thief, and I'm not surprised to see the apple hasn't fallen far from the tree."

'A thief!' Kat was floored, but she didn't know whether to defend herself or kick the lady off her property. Before she could decide, Ida had her cell phone to her ear. From the one side of the conversation she could hear, Kat realized she was calling the police.

'Fine. Call them,' Kat thought, rolling her eyes. It didn't bother her only in the sense she had done nothing wrong. She went on tending to the other customers, making change for their purchases, and helping them find what they were looking for as if there hadn't been an exchange between her and the woman calling 911.

The truth was it did bother her. It upset her a lot. She was new in Fogpoint in a way. No one really knew who she was except that she was Dot Libby's niece. That familial connection alone carried a lot of weight and cast a shadow over her as her aunt's eccentricities were well known. This wasn't the first impression she'd hoped to make for herself.

Ten to fifteen minutes passed before a patrol car pulled up, and two officers emerged from it. They walked up to the sale together and loudly asked for Ida Rothstein. They wouldn't have had to as she was trying to weave around the gawkers, making a bee line straight to them.

"That's me!" she announced, standing a couple feet to the side of one of them.

Kat forced herself to look away and let her carry on with her complaint. The officers would make their way to her soon enough. Most of the customers had been present when Ida called her a thief, but a few were new.

"What's going on over there?" a man asked, nodding his head in her direction.

"I didn't have what she was looking for," Kat said, shaking her head. "Apparently, it's an arrestable offense."

The man chuckled. "Nor me, but I reckon I'll just wait a bit till your next sale," he said with a wink.

It was becoming clear most everyone was showing up with not just a wish list, but a list of expected finds. She crossed one arm across her chest and used it to support the elbow of her other arm while she pinched her lower lip between her thumb and forefinger. *'Why did Aunt Dot have all these people's things?'* she wondered. They couldn't have been stolen because the police would've been involved a long time ago.

"Ma'am," a male voice interrupted her thoughts.

Kat snapped to and looked at who was talking. The man was dressed in the signature dark blue uniform, and his badge read D. Billings. "Yes," she sighed.

"I'm Officer Billings with the FHPD. How are you doing today?" he asked.

"You tell me," she smiled, giving a side eye to Ida. The woman was too far away for Kat to hear her clearly, but her arms were wildly moving through the air as she animatedly spoke with the other officer.

The policeman laughed and nodded. "Yeah, I bet. So anyway, can you tell me what happened? We've spoken with Mrs. Rothstein, but I'm afraid we can't quite make heads nor tails of it."

Kat removed the elastic which was binding her ponytail on top of her head, and she shook her hair out before using her fingers to pull it up again and rewrap the elastic around the base. "She came here looking for a specific silver flatware set. When I told her I didn't have one for sale, she became irate. Called the police and accused me of being a thief."

Finishing with her hair, she crossed her arms, looking at Ida's back. The other officer was talking to her now, and Ida's stance said more than words about how she felt. She had hunched a bit since the last time Kat looked her way and was shaking her head. Ida's hands balled into small fists, relaxed and balled up again.

"Well, we don't think you're a thief," the officer grinned.

He was trying to ease the tension of the situation. Kat appreciated it, but she couldn't force a smile in return.

"Officer Wilson is explaining to her there's nothing we can do if you don't want to sell the silver," he went on.

Kat straightened up and narrowed her eyes. "Don't want to?" she asked. "There isn't any," she said, looking around at what was left of everything she drug from the house that morning. It was shocking how much had already sold.

Officer Billings nodded toward the house. "None at all?" he asked.

"I don't know," she said. "There might be. I haven't gone through everything yet. Why is she so insistent I have the exact set she's looking for anyway?"

"You don't know?" he asked.

Kat simply shook her head. The stress of the last few months, primarily the last couple of weeks were taking its toll. She felt a good decade older and had a form of exhaustion she couldn't shake even with a good night's sleep.

"Huh." The detective raised an eyebrow and nodded his head from side to side like he was considering what she said. "Interesting."

She dropped her arms to the side and ducked her head, trying to get directly in front of the officer's face. There was nothing interesting about this woman causing such a scene for her, and she was confident her aunt hadn't stolen anything either.

"Her mom gave it to your aunt years ago," he said.

"Gave it to her?" Kat asked.

The officer shrugged, "Gave it or sold it. Not really sure. Either way, it had been in the family for a long time, and now that your aunt is…" He stopped abruptly realizing how the sentence was shaping up.

"Dead," Kat said point blank.

"Has passed away," he finished. "She thought she might be able to get it back. Buy it back," he added.

Kat rubbed her temples with her fingers. "I'd sell it to her. I would. There is a lot to go through in that house," she said. "This," she emphasized, motioning at what was left in the driveway, "is what I'm selling today."

"Understandable. Might I suggest a notebook? Keep track of any specifics in case you come across it later," Officer Billings said.

"Sure," Kat agreed. What she really wanted to say was I would have sold it to her had she not pulled this stunt, but she'd be the bigger person. She'd take down Ida's information just in case.

The officer wrote down Ida's information for Kat because the woman refused to speak to her again. That might make a future sale difficult. It didn't take long until the officers were leading Ida down the driveway, away from the sale, to her car. After she was on her way, the officers waved once more and left. They should've stuck around a little longer.

Less than thirty minutes passed before Kat's next irate visitor. He looked young enough to still be in high school, and he was searching for a painting.

Kat didn't catch the specifics and cut him off before he could go into detail. There were no paintings in this sale. Kat explained she hadn't come across any she wanted to part with yet, but there was much more to go through in the house. She offered him the notebook to write down his information, and she'd call him if she came across it. More than one page had already been filled out by various customers searching for something specific. It was going well. He was polite and well mannered. No fuss at all until he was about to leave.

"It's not right that you're doing this," he said angrily.

"Doing what?"

The young man's temper flared. His face reddened, and he spat as he enunciated the words he shot at her. "You're nothing more than a thief!"

'Here we go again.'

Everyone around them stopped and stared. The yard sale was turning into public theater with regular free shows to entertain them.

"Same as your aunt," he added. Turning to the other customers, he asked, "Who else is hoping to find their lost valuables here? Their family heirlooms? Anything that might have been worth its weight that was hocked to that thieving old witch?"

Kat's head snapped to attention, and she tried to focus on him rather than the gathering crowd. There was a low rumble of collective whispers, and she could see nods of agreement from her peripheral vision. "Leave," she told him sternly.

The man stared at her for several long moments, neither of them conceding. "I'm sorry. What?" The man finally spoke.

A hush had fallen over the curious onlookers, and Kat sighed. She expected her customers would be here mostly out of curiosity, and yes, she half expected there to be some comments or snide remarks about her aunt. Being accused of witchcraft was absurd, but no one was going to accuse her family of being dishonest thieves.

Dorothy Libby marched to the beat of her own drum and always had. She stood out which put a target for ridicule on her back. Kat had hoped to fit in, or better yet, fly under the radar during the year she had to live in Fogpoint Harbor. After this gossip circulated the town, there wouldn't be a chance of that.

"I told you to leave," she repeated, unblinking as she stared at him.

"No," the man said, backing up and looking at the audience he had amassed.

Kat was afraid of this. She couldn't physically remove him from her property. Not only was his size too large for her to make the attempt, but his age was the bigger issue. The last thing she needed was to try to force him off her driveway only to discover she had assaulted a minor. If he didn't leave voluntarily and no one present came to her aid, encouraging him to go which it didn't seem was likely to happen, her only option was a police escort. Having the cops at her sale twice wasn't something she cared to endure.

"Please, sir," she said calmly. "I'd like you to leave." When the rumors ran rampant, no one better say she was hot headed.

"No," the man said defiantly. He kicked at a small pebble with his foot then looked at her smiling. "I'm not going to leave. What I am going to do is report you on behalf of all the residents of Fogpoint for selling stolen goods." He pulled out his phone and dialed 911 before putting it to his ear.

And there it was. The cops would be back in a matter of minutes. They might not have made it farther than a few blocks since they left. The sale was over. Kat began packing up what she had just finished setting out on the tables, filling in the holes created by previous sales. People clambered to her to pay for the items they'd been contemplating purchasing.

The boxes and bags she'd carried out of the house a few hours ago had been broken down and stuffed into one remaining box that would go straight to the recycle bin. There was even one tote only partially full. The sale had been going well all morning aside from a couple unruly customers, but seeing the empty containers, she realized just how much she'd sold. She was putting the last of the items into a tote when the police walked up again. Some of the other customers were hanging around, or deliberately walking slowly away in an attempt to eavesdrop as long as possible.

"We meet again," Billings said, offering a warm smile.

Kat couldn't bring herself to return it. The day had been entirely too taxing, and it wasn't even noon. She nodded toward the young man who had called for the police only to find Officer Wilson was already speaking with him.

"What is it this time?" Billings asked. "More flatware?"

The young man was excitedly waving his arms about, pointing in her direction often, as he spoke with the other officer. Kat was watching them closely, and barely heard what Officer Billings said to her. It took a minute for the words to get through her thoughts.

"No, a painting," she sighed. She carefully laid one table on its side and folded the legs for storage.

"Do you have it?" he asked.

Kat glanced at him, trying to see a hidden meaning in what he said. She shook her head slowly. "This morning, I would've said I don't know, but the chances would be slim. By the time Ida came along, I would've said I might, but I haven't gone through everything yet."

Billings stepped forward and helped her with the next table. "What about now? What would you say?"

She looked up at the house, at what was once her aunt's bedroom window, hoping somehow Aunt Dot could provide the answers she needed. "I guess I'd say add your name to the list, and I'm sure I'll find it eventually."

The officer pulled one corner of his mouth up in a wry smile and nodded. "I didn't think it'd take long for you to figure it out," he said.

Kat wondered what he was alluding to. Just because it was obvious her aunt had a house filled with junk, valuable or otherwise that had once belonged to people in the town did not mean she had figured anything out. If anything, she was more confused about who her aunt was, her family, and the house she inherited than she had been the morning the lawyer called her at work to break the news her Aunt Dot had passed away for the second time in her life.

No further details were ever provided. Officer Wilson joined their conversation before she could say anything more. "Packing up?" he asked.

"Yeah," she nodded. "It's been too eventful a morning for my taste," she admitted.

"In the future, give us a heads up, and we'll have the calls fielded better to have anyone with grievances come down to the station instead of interrupting your sale," he suggested.

"Thanks," Kat forced a smile. There would be no more sales. The future of her aunt's hoarding was still up in the air. She'd hate to toss so much that was in perfectly good condition, but she didn't have the patience or the follow through to list it all online either.

The officers left and with them, the rest of the crowd dispersed too. Kat drug the tables back to the garage and leaned them on the side. There wouldn't be a free space to store them unless she pulled them into the dining room. She closed her eyes and twirled a lock of hair around her finger. There was always the option of hiring someone to clear everything out. She could afford it thanks to her aunt, but she wanted to go through it all first in the hopes of accidentally stumbling across something that would resolve all the mysteries forming since her aunt's death. Maybe there would be a map on the back of one of the paintings with a giant red X to mark the spot. She laughed at the image in her head.

"Excuse me," a voice called out.

Kat jumped and turned to see a well-dressed middle aged man standing near the totes she had packed up. She wondered how long he'd been there, how long she'd been lost in her thoughts of the work she had to do. He'd seen her laughing at nothing and probably assumed she was as crazy as her aunt.

"Sorry," she said, walking toward him. "The sale is over."

The man didn't take his eyes off the totes. "Over? Seems like there's a lot left."

'You don't know the half of it,' she thought.

"I'd like to take it all off your hands," he said, finally lifting his head to look at her. "My name is Kenneth Sampson," he said, extending his hand. "I own 'Time Well Spent' on the shore road across from the beach."

Kat shook his hand. It wasn't a store she was familiar with, but a lot had changed since her last visit.

"I own two other stores with my wife and son. I mostly dabble in antiques, but we sell other used items from more recent eras you don't see every day," he explained. "I'm always looking for new stock."

"How much stock do you need?" Kat asked, crossing her arms. Mr. Sampson might be the answer to most of her problems.

The two of them talked at length about the state of her aunt's house and what might be found hidden within those walls. They agreed to a monthly schedule where Kenneth would come and haul away a load, regardless of what it contained. Anything he couldn't use at one of his stores would be up to him to get rid of one way or another.

Kat killed time waiting for him to return with his trailer to load up what was already out of the house. She walked the empty boxes to the bin on the curb and pulled the tables onto the porch. They'd have to take up space in the hallway until she cleared a better place for storage.

From the corner of her eye, she saw a figure rummaging through the totes waiting in the driveway and wondered how she hadn't heard Kenneth pull up. As she turned to head over to him, she realized it wasn't the same man. The stranger in the driveway was taller, and she could tell his build was muscular under the suit he wore. His sandy brown hair was nicely trimmed, and she could see a peak of his tan between the collar of his jacket and the bottom of his hairline when he leaned over a tote.

There was still a few feet separating them when he heard her approach. His head tilted down and to the side when he noticed her. The man turned around, and even from this distance, she was taken in by his sparkling green eyes. The world spun around her and took her breath away.

'*No,*' she told herself. '*One year, and I'm gone. There can be nothing holding me in Fogpoint.*'

Chapter Ten
First Date

KAT PACED NERVOUSLY near the front room windows. With every pass toward the door, she would glance out at the driveway then reprimand herself for it, lecturing herself not to do it again. The next pass her eyes would still shift to see if any cars were coming up the drive like they took orders from no one, not even the brain which controlled their movements. This had been going on since she finished getting ready far earlier than she needed to, and she didn't see an end in sight.

She stopped in the hallway near the front door and groaned in frustration, batting her legs gently with her fists. "No," she said out loud. "This is not why you're here. This was not a part of the plan." Ever since agreeing to this date, she had regretted it. There was no optimal outcome.

If things worked out with him, it wouldn't end well. Her life was not in Fogpoint, and she doubted very much he always dreamed of moving away. The townies, as her aunt had always called the residents, loved this life. They wanted to stay by the water where eight months of the year life was normal. It was only chaos in the summertime when the tourists descended.

The money they spent and the stories the townies shared about them over coffee every morning was enough to get them through till the next season.

Chances were Dante was not the love of her life. It only worked this way in movies where a woman would have a serendipitous encounter with her soul mate when she was least expecting it. *'Least expecting? No, more like not on the market till I get back home.'*

She ran her hands along the front of her light purple sundress, smoothing out wrinkles that didn't exist. Her aunt would've loved the floral print, and it just dawned on her it was probably the reason she packed it. The dress was cute. It was sweet how it reminded her of Aunt Dot, but there were far better options which had been hanging in her closet back home when she was deciding what to pack away in storage for a year and what was coming with her to Fogpoint.

Maybe she should've bought something new to wear. Her mind was drawing a blank over what fabrics and colors would be better in a situation like this. Even with the cool breeze blowing in through the windows, Kat felt like she was sweating buckets. It wasn't even hot out by anyone's standards.

'Stop!' If the date bombed, she'd have rejection to face. If it went well, she just added another complication to her life. It was already more difficult than calculous, and once upon a time, Kat sincerely believed nothing would ever trip her up more than that class had.

'He's late,' she thought, glancing at her watch. She shook her head and continued her pacing. It wasn't even seven yet. There were still several minutes left before he'd even be considered on time. *'Just because you're ready doesn't mean he*

should be.'

Kat maintained her pacing up and down the hall and gave up trying to be still. She stumbled into the hallway table as she turned and grimaced. *'That's going to leave a mark,'* she thought, massaging her hip. Better to get the nervous energy out now then have it gnawing at her while she was out with him. It was a better path for her nerves. While she could see out the windows on the other side of the door, most of the driveway was blocked from view. She didn't walk all the way to the door, forcing herself to stop at the edge of the entryway and turn around.

'This is ridiculous.'

"Why are you so anxious?" She angrily asked the doorway to the kitchen. This wasn't her first date. There had been other dates with good looking men who made her heart leap into her stomach with a single glance. Something was different this time. She had been on pins and needles with jittery excitement ever since Dante asked her out two days ago at the end of her first sale.

Kat had almost completed another pass back to the end of the hall when she heard the unmistakable sound of a car door closing. Her heart thumped so hard she worried she might have to skip dinner and go straight to the emergency room. She stared straight ahead frozen in place, listening to footsteps on the porch followed by the chime of the doorbell.

There was a brief sway in the room, and her arms flew into the air instinctively, reaching for something to hold onto out of fear she might pass out. *'Stop it!'* Her mind yelled.

She took a couple deep breaths and walked to the door slowly forcing her feet to move, having to teach herself to walk again with every step. With a deep breath she opened the door and instantly melted into a smile when Dante's green eyes sparkled at her.

"Wow. You're breathtaking," he said.

Kat felt the heat rise in her cheeks and glanced down coyly before saying, "Thank you." His smile was mesmerizing, and if she didn't force her eyes away, she'd do nothing but stare at his face.

"These are for you." He held out a bouquet of white daisies.

They were her favorite, but he couldn't have known that. She took them from him and lifted them close to her face, inhaling their sweet scent. "Thank you," she said. "Come in while I put these in a vase."

As she walked to the kitchen, she felt him watching her. Each step was awkward like her legs still hadn't learned what to do. At the sink, she glanced over her shoulder quickly to see if he had followed her, but he wasn't there. She breathed a sigh of relief and shook her head. She set about grabbing a vase and clippers to trim the stems while mentally coaching herself to get it together. She carried the vase down the hall to place it on the table where her aunt had always displayed fresh lilacs and found Dante staring into the front room.

He took a deep breath and turned to her. "Fond memories," he said. "Ready?"

Kat picked up her purse off the table and hung the thin strap on her shoulder. "Yes." She was as ready as she'd ever be.

Dante navigated the streets like a true townie. They didn't say much during the drive which gave Kat's overactive anxiety plenty of time to rule the date a complete disaster when it had barely begun. She recognized the restaurant he stopped at, but she couldn't quite remember having ate there. A nagging thought just out of reach in her mind told her she had. It was possible she had come there with Aunt Dot at some point. Her aunt was a creature of habit, but on occasion, they stopped somewhere new.

It had an unpresuming exterior nestled between a small gallery for local artists and a clothing boutique. In fact if you didn't already know there was a restaurant behind those doors, you would be surprised to learn there was. It didn't draw much traffic from the tourists like the bright and modern joints closer to the shore. It was more of a well-kept secret, and the locals wanted to keep it that way.

'Of course, its seafood,' she thought. It wasn't her favorite. Shrimp and crab were about all she would eat. Maybe if she had grown up out here it'd be different, or if she had a few summers for her aunt to introduce her to more of the local fare.

They walked in and were seated near the windows looking out at the street. If they had been on the other side of the restaurant, Kat might have noticed something familiar about the paintings hung along the wall.

After they were seated at their table, Dante said, "I hope this place is to your liking. Have you been here before?"

Kat stifled her opinions about seafood and smiled at him. "It seems familiar, but if I've ever been here, it was when I was little. I don't remember."

"You'll love it," he assured her. "Everything is delicious."

They looked over the menu and placed their order without speaking any more. While waiting on the appetizer, the lingering doubts forced themselves to the forefront of Kat's mind once again. Silence couldn't be a good indication the evening was going well.

This wasn't typically like her at all. She'd chew anyone's ear off, even a stranger. It had to be Fogpoint affecting her. This town and its experiences with her aunt made her insecure in a way she'd previously never faced.

"So," Dante began. It was more to break the silence than from having anything to say.

"How did you know my aunt?" Kat blurted out quickly before he could continue his thought.

Dante chuckled softly, placing his elbows on the table and rubbed his hands together before clasping them. "I did promise to tell you about your aunt," he said, "but I thought we'd save the hard hitting stuff for later."

The expression on Kat's face fell, and he must have caught it.

"No, its fine," he said, looking her in the eye. "We can discuss Dorothy now."

It was weird hearing her aunt called by her full first name. The only times she had heard it used was when her mom was frustrated with her aunt and when the lawyer got in touch regarding the estate. Kat didn't mention it. She sat patiently and waited for him to continue.

"When I was in college, my dad died unexpectedly."

"I'm sorry." The words slipped out from habit.

He waved his hand, but quietly said, "Thank you."

Dante straightened up and took a sip. "I came and went through the house, but I didn't know what I was looking for, much less where to look. I was trying to find any important documents or account information. I didn't even know if he had a will."

"A friend of mine suggested making a visit to the Libby house, so I called your aunt who told me to stop by whenever I was able. I went there the next morning, and she sat me in the family room. Before I could say a word, she said what I needed was in an envelope taped to the back of the headboard."

Kat narrowed her eyes. It didn't seem possible for her aunt to have that knowledge unless she was close to Dante's dad. The journal flashed in her mind, but that was ridiculous, but not nearly as absurd as Aunt Dot being close enough to someone in Fogpoint for them to tell her their secrets.

"After that," Dante went on, "she mostly checked up on me. She asked how I was doing and about school. Your aunt was very concerned about if I would stay in school. It felt nice to be looked after like that, more like a grandmother might do, you know?"

She wasn't sure how to answer that, so she nodded instead. She never knew her grandparents. Aunt Dot was as close as she came to having any.

"When I went home, I pulled out my dad's bed, and sure enough." Dante shook his head like he still didn't believe it all these years later. "There was a giant envelope containing everything I had searched frantically through the house trying to find the previous day."

"How did she know where it was?" Kat asked. "Was she a friend of your dads?"

Dante laughed like she told a joke. "You truly don't know?" He asked when he realized Kat was being serious.

Kat half shrugged and looked away. It wasn't that she didn't know; she was still struggling to accept it.

"You're not the only occupant of your aunt's house," Dante

said.

"I'm beginning to understand now." She slowly nodded not realizing she was doing it.

He had a lot more to share throughout dinner about her aunt. He visited her often, and she filled him with updates about Kat whenever he was there. "She was awful proud of you, you know? She always rambled on incessantly like you were her favorite subject. You were all she'd talk about if you let her."

The card she found from her mom sent shortly before she died must not have been the only communication between the two women over the years. Kat wished more than ever she had known her aunt had been alive all that time. Listening to Dante's stories about her aunt made her realized in a way she hadn't fathomed before how valuable her aunt's wisdom and insight would've benefited her as an adult. It renewed her sadness for the years lost and made her regret not taking a trip to Fogpoint after reaching adulthood.

She'd thought about it often. It wouldn't have taken much to make the drive out and spend a couple nights in a motel. There was a list of places she wanted to visit which were special to her memories of her aunt. She'd take a tour, enjoy the beach, and drive by her aunt's house. Sometimes when she daydreamed the trip she would knock on the door and explain how she used to summer there, hoping the new owner wouldn't mind if she walked the back of the property to the cove. It was highly unlikely she would've gone that far, but maybe she would've found the courage.

Even if she hadn't, there's always the possibility she would've run into her aunt around town. She could've come face to face with her long before she passed if she had ever got around to making the drive. The only thing she had in Fogpoint was her Aunt Dot which meant Fogpoint had died with her. It would be something she regretted not doing for a long time to come.

"I'm sorry," Dante said. "Your aunt's only recently passed away. I'm sure it's still fresh for you. Here I've been going on and on about her for close to an hour."

"It's alright," Kat assured him. "It's not that."

He looked at her questioningly, but didn't press the subject. "It's why I came to the sale."

Kat was puzzled. She looked up at him not understanding what he meant.

"It was because of how much she talked about you. I felt like I already knew you. That's why I had to meet you. I had to put a face to the name."

Kat's breath caught in her throat. *'What does he know?'*

Chapter Eleven
Obvious Explanations

KAT HADN'T SEEN DETECTIVE Kinley since the day he took her to the scene of Harold's death. Every morning, he'd send a message asking if there was any news from the house. Each time, she'd answer the same with, "Nothing yet."

Part of her was fascinated by how he so freely believed in the supernatural, but she realized that belief might not have been easily formed. There might have been a time when he'd chalk this kind of talk up to nonsense and nothing more. It made her curious what happened to change that attitude. Maybe someday she'd ask how a detective came to accept the aide of supposed ghosts during an investigation.

It was no surprise the house didn't have much to say not since the night she made a fool out of herself asking it to talk when she returned from the crime scene. There had been a message later that night, but nothing more since. The last words written in the journal weren't very climatic by comparison.

"Harold was murdered."

"His grandson did it."

"Find the specks."

There was nothing other than the notes in the journal. Nothing was moved around. Unexplained noises didn't keep her awake with the covers pulled tight over her head hoping the woven cotton polyester blend would create a force shield even formless spirits couldn't pass through. A dark energy, or any energy at all was never felt.

The only evidence of spirit activity was three simple rounds of automatic writing which was hardly proof. Even the staunchest believer would require more before confirming a haunting. It wouldn't be necessary because Kat could explain it simply and easily.

It was the day after her run in with Harold at the café when the words, "Harold was murdered," appeared in the journal. Kat wasn't one who typically wished ill upon others even in the direst of circumstances. For her to accept those words came straight from her subconscious thoughts was difficult, but nowhere near as challenging as accepting the house was haunted at face value.

She had been overly stressed and emotional. There had been so much to do since meeting with the lawyer and very little time to get it all done. Everything was put on the back burner. There hadn't been a chance to process how she felt about learning her aunt had been alive all those years, reconcile with the fact her mom had lied to her for most of her life, let alone think about where the inheritance came from in the first place. Her aunt certainly never lived life as though she were wealthy.

Harold was simply the most recent straw on an already over loaded camel's back. She didn't really mean the wishful thinking she wrote in the journal without paying attention to what she was writing. It was more symbolic. She merely wished an end to all the "Harold's" in her life. Anything which caused her added worry or anxiety, to feel weighted down, or stressed was represented in those words. She saw it as an affirmation to herself from then forward, she would put it all behind her to get through this.

Then came the next phantom phrase. "His grandson did it," was pretty obvious too. In all murder cases, the spouse and immediate family were the number one suspects. They were usually ruled out before anyone was else was investigated. While she sat at the desk thinking about the events of the morning with the journal and what Kinley had to say, her mind's wheels were spinning, trying to figure it out. A process which was probably brought on by Kinley's offer of a job. She had jumped the gun and went into work mode using what she'd picked up watching true crime shows over the years.

Why she chose a grandson over anyone else was something she couldn't explain. It was easy to analyze it now with all of society's typically expected sexisms and ageist thoughts attached to it. It's hard for people to accept women are capable of murder, especially when it occurs up close and personal. They seem women as poisoning their victim or possibly shooting them. It's a gross underestimate, but one her subconscious made as well assuming the killer was a male.

A grandson would have youth on his side over a middle aged man. That isn't limited to energy or strength, but is more directed toward the underdeveloped mind. The downfall of most youth is the inability to think things through. They act rashly without consideration to the consequences. All of this must've been what played out her decision to name the grandson.

The reality was she had no knowledge about Harold or his family. She wouldn't have known if he ever had children much less grandchildren. It was a shot in the dark guess. It was harder to explain how her hand wrote something out a second time. Once was stress and an overwhelmed emotionally ragged mind, but the second one was pushing it. Detective Kinley had already mentioned something about the house speaking to her. Add that to her frazzled state, and it was really no surprise she did it again.

The third set of words was the easiest of all to explain. "Find the specks." It had to refer to the specks of blood at the crime scene. She had already found them, well discovered the lack of them where something had been sitting during the attack. This one was the best proof she had it was her all along guiding the words on the paper. Ghosts wouldn't tell her something she already knew if they did, in fact, exist and were, in fact, helping her to solve the case.

"Ugh!" Kat threw the roll of tape across the room she had been using to seal boxes. The end piece had collapsed on the roll, and she couldn't get her nail under it to peel it off.

"Haunted," she sighed, standing up. She could explain the notes in the journal a hundred different ways, and they'd never make as much sense as spirit writing did. Occam's razor indicates the simplest explanation is the likeliest. While she could go off on a tangent about deep seeded emotional traumas and the subconscious mind exerting itself, she could also simply assert, "The spirits in the house communicate through me using automatic writing." It wasn't exactly what was meant by Occam's, but she still felt it applied.

Kat found the roll of tape where it came to a stop under the desk across the room and brought it back to the pile of boxes. It was her last one, and she didn't feel like leaving the house tonight to buy more. Mr. Sampson would be by tomorrow to pick up what she had ready. These boxes didn't have to go then, but she wanted to unload the junk lying around as quickly as possible. It'd be a couple more weeks before his next pick up.

After several more failed attempts, she gave up on the tape. Sampson would have to take the boxes as is, and she hoped it wouldn't be an issue. One by one she carried them out of the spare bedroom and down the stairs. When she headed out of the room with the last box in her arms, her foot caught the leg of the bed, tripping her and propelling her forward into the wardrobe.

It lunged backward and banged the wall, but luckily, it didn't rock back forward. Something fell inside it. Kat heard it shimmy down the wall which surprised her since she had already cleared all the contents, but when she opened the doors, it was still empty from when she sorted through the hanging clothes earlier.

Kat had been struggling with the decision of selling the furniture or leaving it for staging when the time came to sell. It was all in excellent condition and very old. Some of the pieces were valuable antiques. It could incentivize an offer. If the furniture caused one more injury to her clumsy frame, it was all going.

Her ankle smarted from the accident, and she limped through the room marveling at how much space she had to do so compared to when she first entered the room before noon.

Slowly, she added her weight to it and eased into working it out. It wasn't a bad injury, but if she babied it, the pain would last a lot longer.

The contents of the box had spilled out onto the floor. Kat glared at the roll of tape, ultimately blaming it for her current situation. She lowered herself next to the box and righted it before piling everything back inside. As she did so, she noticed the edge of something sticking out from behind the wardrobe.

She set the box on the bed and bent along the wall to grab whatever it was hidden away. It must've been what she heard fall. It would've been on top of the wardrobe hidden by the decorative border along the front when she fell into it.

Kat retrieved the large manila envelope and sat on the edge of the bed. It was thick, but nothing had been written on the outside to label it. She opened it, carefully ripping through the tape covering the flap while trying not to damage the contents inside in case it contained anything important. She reached inside and removed a large stack of papers.

The ones on top appeared to be medical records of some sort for a Jillian Libby. Aunt Dot's granddaughter had passed away after a long illness, so she thumbed through everything to see if that's all this was. There was a legal notice. Both Jillian and Aunt Dot's names were mentioned in it, but Kat didn't have time to read it.

The sound of the doorbell interrupted her. *'Who could that be?'* It was probably Kinley. That was the only person she could think of who might have reason to drop by. He might be growing frustrated from her lack of information on the case. *'Maybe he wants to try talking to the house,'* she snickered.

She tossed the envelope and stack of papers on the bed.

Something nagged at her memory about Jillian's death. It had been long forgotten, and it was entirely possible she didn't fully understand what was being said at the time. Children can't always make heads or tails of grown up conversations until they're older. It was clicking somewhere in her mind the death had been a result of poor medical care or rather a mistake on the part of a doctor.

Kat picked up the box once more and tried to remember exactly what is was about Jillian as she carried it down the stairs, but nothing was coming to her. She added the box to the rest of the ones waiting for Sampson's visit in the morning.

There was a figure on the porch, and she could tell by the outline it wasn't Kinley. It had been a long day. She was exhausted and didn't have the energy to deal with whoever might be stopping by. No one had been especially welcoming so far, and she couldn't imagine the stranger outside was here for anything good.

For now, she'd slip down the hall into the kitchen. It was time to eat, and she could ignore whoever it was without risk of being seen through the windows back there. She turned into the stack of boxes she'd already forgotten about and practically fell on her face. "Ow! Shoot!" She grabbed onto the stair rail to steady herself.

'So much for pretending not to be home. What would I be if not a klutz?' She stacked the boxes again still debating if she should answer the door or not. *'Maybe they'll think it was the ghosts.'* The thought made her smile.

"Kat?" The door knob rattled as the person outside tried to open it. "Katrina! Are you okay?"

She stared at the door like it had just appeared in front of her, and she'd never seen it till now. That voice was familiar.

"Kat!" He was becoming more frantic and pounding on the door now with the flat of his hand.

"Dante?" She unlocked the door and swung it open. He looked handsome in the light of late day, dressed casually in jeans and a t-shirt.

He looked her up and down then around her down the hall. "What happened?"

"I tripped. What are you doing here?"

Dante continued to peer around her before deciding everything looked fine. "Oh, I..." He looked side to side then found the bag he dropped and picked it up. "I thought I'd take a chance you might be home," he said, holding up the bag.

Kat could see the tub of ice cream and whipped topping through the nearly transparent plastic. It would be a great way to end the day, but she hadn't had anything to eat yet. *I'm old enough to have ice cream for dinner if I want,* she reminded herself.

"I should've called first," Dante's expression dropped. He mistook her slow response to mean she wasn't interested.

She smiled at him and stepped aside. "Not at all. I could use something sweet right now."

Dante came inside, eyeing the boxes with a questioning look.

"Sampson is making a pick up in the morning," she said, motioning to him to follow her down the hall.

"You should've said something. I would've helped you."

Kat waved him off, shaking her head as she walked into the kitchen. It wasn't pride or any other reason she didn't ask for help except she didn't know what she might find. "It gives me something to do."

She pulled bowls from the cabinets and silverware from the drawer then stood by and watched while Dante made the sundaes. "Did you ever meet my aunt's granddaughter Jillian?" After the question was out, she realized Jillian would've died long before he met her aunt when he was in college. "Never mind. Did my aunt ever talk about her?"

"All the time," he laughed. He shook his head and stared off like he was remembering their conversations. "I think you are the only person she rambled on about more than Jill."

It was bittersweet having this connection. She was thankful to have met someone who knew her aunt during the years she wasn't around, but it still made her wish she could've continued to be a part of her life too.

"Do you know how she died?"

"Died?" Dante stuck the serving spoon in his mouth and closed the ice cream, handing it to her to put away. He ate the ice cream off the spoon and put it in the sink. "I don't remember hearing your aunt talk about her death. No. I'm sorry."

Chapter Twelve
Case Files

KAT STOOD IN THE OPEN back door and stared at the wooded area out back. Part of her wished Dante hadn't dropped by as much as she enjoyed his company. Their conversation had taken an interesting turn, and she couldn't get it out of her head.

There was a much needed trip to the library in the very near future. Dante couldn't remember much of the details, but the land this house sat on was rich in history. It might explain why the walls could talk.

She shut the door and walked through the house to grab her purse and leave. It would have to wait for another day. Kinley was expecting her in twenty minutes. After a week of not having any information to give him, she finally broke down and told him what the journal said the day he came by and introduced himself.

"His grandson did it."

Kinley didn't say much in response. He didn't ask for more details or explain why the department had already ruled the family out as suspects. All he asked was for a meeting with her, face to face, to look over the files.

Kat walked through the police station door with barely a moment to spare. *'If you're on time, you're late.'* The voice inside her head pulled that old gem out of somewhere. She couldn't remember when she'd ever heard someone say it, but there it was.

She glanced around, but didn't see the detective. He hadn't said he'd meet her near the entrance again, but she had expected to see him hanging around waiting for her like the last time. She pressed the call button for the elevator and hoped it wouldn't take too long.

The doors opened, and the detective was standing inside. "Miss Thompson," he greeted with a smile. "Right on time. I like that."

He stepped to the side and Kat entered. "How have you been?" he asked, pressing the button for the floor below.

Kat inhaled deeply and smiled. "Good," she said. "And you?"

The detective shook his head. "Getting nowhere fast, but other than that, I can't complain."

She wasn't sure, but she felt like it was a dig about the case. It wasn't her fault she wasn't qualified for this line of work.

They walked down the hall to his office. It looked like it had been straightened up since the last time she was there. The expression on her face gave away her thoughts.

"Yeah, I cleaned," he laughed. "Or tried to anyway."

"It looks good," Kat said. There was still some clutter stacked away in the corners, but it was a far cry better than it had been.

Kinley motioned to the chairs across the desk from him.

They didn't need to be cleared before she could sit down this time. "So," he clapped his hands together. "His grandson, huh?"

"That's right," Kat nodded.

"Didn't happen to say which one?"

Kat's eyes widened. It never occurred to her there might be more than one grandson to consider.

He leaned back and braced his hands against the desk. "I was afraid of that. Well, let's get going then."

On the floor behind the desk was a box, and he grabbed a couple files and a steno pad from it. One by one, he gave Kat a rundown of the grandchildren. Murphy had one child, a daughter, and she had three sons. All were well into adulthood, and all had alibis.

"You don't think you could ask for a name?" Kinley asked.

Kat chuckled then realized he wasn't joking. "I don't think it works that way. Actually, I don't know how it works."

"The oldest lives in the Midwest. I'm pretty sure he checks out. The other two? Well, their alibis are weak at best. See what you can do," he said, pushing everything across the desk.

"Me?" Kat's eyes widened in surprise, and her eyes darted around the room searching for an escape plan.

"Yeah, that's why you're here, to pick up the case notes and check into them."

Kat didn't move a muscle. She stared at the files. Her heart pounded, and she wasn't sure she wanted to be a part of this anymore.

"Why did you think you were coming down here?"

She opened her mouth to speak a couple times before any words came out. Finally, she managed to say, "To talk? Bounce ideas off each other? I thought we'd be looking into this together."

The detective shook his head and stood up. "Sorry, Kat. I've got other cases plus a new one handed to me this morning."

Minutes later, she found herself walking to the car carrying a stack of files along with the legal pad. She wasn't sure which was the smartest choice. It was tempting to politely decline the detective's offer, more like insistence, of taking this home to look over and leave everything in his office. Instead, she went with the only other option she could come up with at the time. Take everything, but do nothing with it once she got to the house.

The feeling of being a fraud was flowing over her in waves along the drive. She'd no sooner push the anxiety down and swallow it when it'd course through her again a few minutes later. It was hard enough working alongside Kinsley, talking with him about the case, but going it alone felt more than wrong. It felt illegal like she had somehow managed to walk out of the police department in front of dozens of officers carrying top secret information she didn't have the security clearance to be informed of its existence much less be given the opportunity to read through them.

As tempting as it was to leave it all in the car and forget about it till tomorrow when she talked with Kinley again, she didn't think it wise. The likelihood of someone randomly breaking into her car on the night she had the files was low, but the possibility of a group of kids sneaking on the property late at night for a better view of the witch house was high.

Kat sighed and wondered if anyone in town actually thought about this place, about her aunt. The sad truth was whatever gossip being shared about Aunt Dot was probably far worse than calling her a witch.

The files didn't make it past the table in the hallway where she dropped them along with her purse and keys. At some point, she might skim through a couple pages to pick up some small detail. When she discussed what she found, if anything, with Kinley, she'd want to make it look like she tried.

It wasn't until much later when she sat at the dining room table eating her dinner when she thought about them again. This was the first room of the house Kat finished cleaning out. That was part of the reason why she spent every minute she could in there. For several days, it was the only room, besides Aunt Dot's bedroom which remained in pristine condition, where she breathed easy without the clutter and mayhem closing in around her, causing her to feel claustrophobic and triggering her anxiety.

The other reason was the painting hanging over the fireplace. Kat had only met one of the five women pictured, but the others were family too. It was reassuring to have Aunt Dot's smiling face watching over her.

While she ate her microwavable lasagna and bowl of veggies barely passing as a salad, the files crept back into her mind. There was no warning to their occupancy of her thoughts. The sudden remembrance of their presence in the hall was all it took to be overcome by them. The harder she tried to forget about them the louder they screamed at her reminiscent of a story about a beating heart she'd read in junior high. Kat carried the soggy tomato and pasta mess she'd been nibbling into the kitchen and gave in to the files.

Sitting in the chair closest to the painting, she read over the clumsy short hand on the legal pad. Maybe with her aunt's painted eyes on the evidence as well, it'd help Kat find some overlooked key piece of information to narrow down which grandson was behind Harold's death. There were three of them to consider.

The oldest was Michael. He had moved out of state not long after getting married. His alibi was the strongest. He had been at work, third shift, the night his grandfather was attacked. It still left the possibility he hired someone. Kinley didn't think the murder was planned. However, if someone had been hired to break in and steal something valuable, Harold could've come home at the wrong time and discovered what was going on.

'*Not very likely,*' Kat told herself. '*If the other two had iron clad alibis, then it'd be something to consider.*'

Adam was a mechanic and definitely had the strength to do it. Kinley said he was an athlete all through high school, very physical, but a knee injury his senior year destroyed his full ride scholarship offers. He went with his second love: engines. He always had a car or bike he'd tinker with in his garage back in school and got a job at a local shop.

He had been with his girlfriend all night. They had gone out, but the part of the date where their whereabouts could be proven had ended at least an hour before the coroner believed Harold had been attacked. They drove around, parked near the beach and talked for a while. He dropped her off around midnight.

'*Talked,*' Kat laughed out loud.

Kat walked into the kitchen and poured a glass of wine. "Technically, he has an alibi," she told the wine glass when she pulled it from the cabinet. It would be easy to lie for him if she believed he was innocent. "Or if she was in on it," Kat said after the first sip touched her soul and ignited her cynicism.

She finished off her glass and poured another one. "It wouldn't be the first time a woman covered for someone she loved." She took another drink and stared out the kitchen window. There had never been anyone in her life she felt so strongly about for her to lie to the police, not that the situation had ever come up with any of her ex-boyfriends. Just thinking about it made her wonder what a love like that felt like, and she felt sorry for herself that she'd probably never find something so special.

The glass was empty again, and she sighed. Leaving both the bottle and the glass in the kitchen was the wise thing to do, but no one ever accused her of being wise. She compromised and left the glass taking only the bottle back to the dining room to continue looking over the files.

Last but not least was David. She pulled a file out from the stack. He was the youngest of the three. He was an artist who owned the small studio next to the restaurant where Dante had taken her for dinner. "Huh, small world."

David went to a state school and majored in art and drama. The studio was opened with a small loan from his grandfather which he paid back in full. He claimed he had stayed late in the studio that night. When he left around ten, he made it almost to his mom's house where he lived before realizing he left his wallet and came back to get it. In his rush, he knocked over a jar of dirty water used to clean brushes, so he cleaned it up before leaving again. The clothes he wore the night before had wet spots on them seen by his mom and had been tested. It wasn't blood. The only proof to his alibi were the alarm codes he entered at the studio. The time stamp on them matched how long it'd take him to drive home and back. His mom verified he got in just before eleven that night.

According to the coroner, the head wound would've occurred between ten and midnight. It was an educated guess. Kat had watched enough crime documentaries to know it wasn't an exact science.

It wasn't just their whereabouts the detectives used to rule them out. There was no motive. This was a close family. There were no feuds or love lost between any of them. No one could come up with any reason for any of the grandchildren to want to hurt him, much less murder him. Harold had always helped them in any way he could.

Of the three grandsons, Kat's suspicion fell on Adam. Michael wasn't in the state and from what she could tell about David, he didn't seem strong enough to inflict a blow like the one Harold endured. Adam was the least successful of the three, and in her opinion, the one most likely to be in need of a loan. If he had come to his grandfather and was denied for the first time, it could be a reason to get angry. They argued, voices raised, and Michael struck him. It wasn't premeditated, but he ran. When his grandfather fell down the stairs, he believed he accidentally killed him and took off out of fear.

Kat needed more than that. She couldn't go to Kinley with a weak guess based on zero evidence and old fashioned beliefs that jocks are more capable of carrying out violence than those interested in the arts.

It also didn't explain what had been against the wall when it occurred. If she could find whatever it was, she could prove her theory. *But how?*

The first step was meeting him. It'd give her a better chance to make the same snap judgment about him. Kat laughed and lifted the bottle to her lips. She was beyond making logical sense now, and that was fine. Her life was on a path all its own and out of her control now. The least she could do was enjoy the ride.

She dug her notepad out from under the mess of files and jotted down a quick note for herself in case hungover Kat forgot what wine loving Kat was thinking when she woke up. *'Walker's Auto Repair,'* she jotted down. It wouldn't hurt to have her brakes checked anyway.

Chapter Thirteen
Brake Check

IT TOOK THREE DAYS before she could get her car in to have the brakes replaced after the initial visit to the shop to have them inspected. Kat had been so gung ho on finding out more about Adam, hoping for some clue which might point to him as being the culprit, she forgot how much she despised mechanics.

Her first visit to Walker's Auto Repair was awful, and she only returned for the benefit of the case. It was a small two bay garage, and the only people she saw were Adam and the owner. She knew it was him by the patch on his coveralls bearing his name, but she wouldn't have had to try to figure out if that was him otherwise. He made his identity clear almost immediately.

When she walked into the office, the owner was the one at the counter, but Adam came in through the side door. "This Ms. Thompson?" he asked.

"Yep," the owner said, hunt and pecking at the keyboard. "She's all yours."

Kat waited while her car was checked out. Her service appointment was for an oil change in addition to the brake check. She'd been meaning to get one since the drive out to Fogpoint. Now was as good a time as any.

The owner disappeared into the shop for a few minutes. When he returned, he tried to convince Kat she should consider replacing her air filter while she was there. He talked on about its condition and how dirty it looked.

Her lips drew into a tight line. "I had it replaced at my last oil change before I moved here," she told him. "I think I'll wait." It happened every time she took her car to a shop.

He didn't say much, but he was trying to maintain the air of being right about his recommendation. Kat picked up one of the magazines next to her chair and flipped through it, hoping her avoidance of him would get his attention off of her. Thankfully, it worked. The hunting magazine she grabbed wasn't exactly keeping her interest.

She was bored in the office and no one else was waiting for service, so she wandered outside near the open bay doors. *'I don't know what I thought I was going to get out of this. If I didn't actually need an oil change, this would be a waste of money.'*

It hadn't been more than a couple minutes before Adam called out to her. "You can come in and watch. We don't mind. It's a slow day."

He said we, but the owner was still in the air conditioned office. Kat wondered how much he'd actually mind over her being so close, but if he had a problem with it, he'd come out and tell her.

Without trying to stare directly at him, she studied him the best she could. He was fit and probably close to six foot tall. It looked like he'd definitely have the strength to hit his grandfather hard enough to knock him down the stairs. That was all the information she was going to get from this though. She glanced around toward the back of the shop where the tall multi drawer tool box sat. It belonged to him. He'd made a trip to it a couple of times plus it had his initials on the inside of the top lid. She wished she could look through it.

'It's not like he stashed the finial he used in it,' she scolded herself.

"So you're the one helping on the case?" Adam's voice broke through the silence between them.

"What?" Kat wasn't trying to play dumb. She'd been lost in her head and didn't quite hear what he asked.

"My grandfather's death," Adam led. When she didn't respond, he asked, "You're Dorothy Libby's relation, right?"

"Yes," Kat said, standing straight. It was becoming her instinct whenever Aunt Dot's name was mentioned. She squared herself to prepare to defend her family from whatever insult was about to be slung at her. "She was my aunt."

Adam's head nod was barely noticeable where he was standing on the far side of her car from her. "I heard you're taking over for her down at the station. That detective said you're assisting on the case."

"That's right," Kat was surprised. She hadn't expected Kinley to have told anyone, especially Harold's family, a novice like herself was involved.

He walked over to her, wiping his hands on a rag. "I believe in all that psychic mumbo jumbo. I know a lot of people think it's a crock. Don't let them get to you."

Kat wasn't expecting this. It was throwing her off her original course. She was certain of the three grandsons, Adam was the most likely suspect. If he was guilty, shouldn't he be suspicious of her suddenly showing up. There were plenty of other garages in Fogpoint where she could've taken her car. Many were nationally recognized chains, cheaper and were able to get you scheduled much quicker than Walker's. This was the type of place townies used to show support for their own, not new residents who barely had a grip on the layout of the streets yet.

'He might be trying to throw me off his scent. Bringing it up himself to try to mirage his innocence.' It could go either way, and she wasn't an expert in deciphering body language or any verbal clues to figure out which way she should lean.

"I don't know how it works or anything, but some people have some kind of ability," he said, tossing the rag over his shoulder. "Like your aunt."

Her eyes widened, and Adam chuckled.

"I guess a lot of people in these parts don't have anything nice to say about her, huh?" he said with a grin.

"You knew my aunt?"

Adam shook his head and went to his tool box. "Not really. Met her a couple times, but that's about it. Most of what I know of her came from my grandpa."

"If you don't mind my asking-"

"Not at all," Adam interrupted. He picked up a carbon copy set of papers from the toolbox and walked back to her. "One thing I learned recently is it helps hearing stories from people who knew the person you lost."

He scratched the side of his head and rolled his eyes to the side. "Grandpa didn't say much about her, but when he did, you could tell he was impressed."

"Harold?" Kat was certain they were talking about two

different people.

Adam nodded. "She'd come in with no leads, no evidence, and march the police straight to the suspect, finding what they needed to convict along the way." He shook his head and chuckled. "It's incredible really, and even my set in his ways grandpa had to give her credit."

"Thank you." Kat meant it. If someone like Harold could appreciate her aunt, at least in private, there was hope for the others in town.

He handed her the paperwork. "Everything's ready. I'll pull the car out front," he said, nodding to the office door.

Kat took the forms and headed to the door of the shop leading to the waiting area.

"You know," Adam said behind her. "I don't think grandpa really believed in anything like psychics or mediums or whatever your aunt was, but he believed in her."

Tears bit at her eyelids, and she sucked in her breath. They couldn't be talking about the same Harold Murphy. Into the office she went, clearing her throat and trying to maintain her composure. There was a lot to digest, and she wouldn't be able to think straight until she was safe in the comfort of her aunt's house, alone.

The earliest time available for her brakes wasn't until Monday mainly because they had to wait on parts. It really was a small town shop. Kat kept nodding her head and trying to encourage the owner to hurry. Every passing second brought her closer to the moment where she might lose it and start bawling.

Finally, she was in her car, heading back to her aunt's house, vowing to never return to Walker's again for any reason. As the weekend went by, she convinced herself it was necessary. She was still torn between whether Adam was full of it and simply trying to blow smoke, or if he really was innocent. Her money was on the former, but she had no way to prove it.

When Monday rolled around, she braced herself to go back, to face whatever curve ball he might throw at her this time. It would be overkill at this point which she believed was proof enough for her even if it wouldn't be for the police department. All she'd have to do next is figure out how to find the evidence she needed to prove it.

He was nowhere to be seen when she arrived. The owner greeted her at the counter again and went over the work order. "Brake pads, rotors, and calipers brings your total to-"

"Just brake pads." Kat was immediately furious.

The old man glanced at her then back at the computer. "I've got you scheduled for everything. That's why we had to wait until today for the parts to get you in."

"I don't know about all that, but it's just the brakes."

"Huh," he muttered. He hit a few more keys then grabbed a stack of papers next to the computer, rifling through them till he found hers. "Says right here on the work order. Did you look at it the last time you were here?"

Kat hadn't, but wasn't about to admit to it. The last thing she wanted to be saddled with was a restocking fee, or something else just as ridiculous. "I don't remember seeing it, but the writing was hard to make out."

He looked at it again and chuckled. "Yeah, I suppose it is. Well, Adam will be back from lunch any minute now, and you can talk it over with him."

He set the paperwork on the counter, and Kat got a clear

view of what it said. It clearly read rotors and calipers underneath what was originally written and in different handwriting. She shook her head and walked to one of the chairs in the empty waiting area. As soon as she sat down, a pickup pulled onto the lot and parked around the side of the building. Two minutes later, Adam walked into the office from the shop.

Adam flashed her a slight smile and nodded hello. The owner gave him the keys to her car and walked out into the shop with him. She could only see the back of Adam's head from where she sat and couldn't hear a word of the conversation. It wasn't hard to figure out the owner was convincing him to talk her into the add-on sales.

After he drove her car into the bay and got it on the lift, he collected her from the office. She didn't have the patience to be jacked around from a mechanic, so she beat him to it. "Replace the rotors, but the calipers are fine."

He chewed the inside of his cheek and stared at the car. "I'll give you my discount," he said. "Parts plus ten percent."

"Thank you."

"Nah, thank you. I know you're going to figure this out. It's the least I can do."

He didn't waste any time going to work on her brakes, and she talked to him around the sound of the tools and air compressor.

"I'm glad you have so much faith in me," she told him.

Adam shrugged. "I believe to an extent, but I also believe the police need all the help they can get. My grandpa didn't have enemies."

This was the second time Kat had heard someone say this

about Harold, and she still had a hard time processing it. "None at all."

"No," he said, removing a tire. "He was a pretty decent guy, always willing to lend a helping hand. You just had to get through the old man stubborn attitude, but he was an easy egg to crack." Adam smiled and laughed at whatever memory ran through his head. "Yeah, people liked him."

'I didn't care for him.'

Kat walked outside and stood near the edge of the road. The street wasn't busy and very few cars passed by while she sorted her thoughts. She wasn't the best judge of character. There were a few ex's in her past who could certainly corroborate that.

Still, nothing about Adam made her think he was the one behind his grandfather's death. Either he was innocent, or he was one heck of an actor. *'I had more motive than Adam did near as I can tell from my one meeting with Harold at the café.'*

When her car was finished, she drove around Fogpoint trying to find some of the local spots her aunt used to take her. Most of the town had changed in the last twenty years. The few places she could remember had been torn down to clear the area for parking or had been changed to some entirely different type of business. Nothing ever stays the same. The world changes constantly, and the only way to survive it is to adapt.

That's what she needed to do now. Her world had changed significantly. This was the new hand life had dealt her. If she was going to make it, even just the rest of this year, she would have to bend and hope she didn't break. That included working for the police. It felt like she had been tossed in the deep end, and there was no one around to save her. It wasn't true. It was her own insecurities getting the best of her. Kinley hadn't thrown her to the wolves and wasn't going to let her make a move he didn't believe she was capable of handling.

It was doubtful David had anything to do with Harold's death either. Kat stopped herself short of thinking the journal had it wrong. Maybe the grandson wasn't the murderer. Maybe he simply did something which set the events in motion to cause it. Whichever grandson it was might not even realize his connection to it yet.

Her car pulled into the drive leading to the Victorian house like it had a mind of its own, leading her there by itself. She nodded as if she agreed with the car's decision. It was time to collect herself and prepare for her next attempt. She would pay David's studio a visit. It still seemed impossible to her for him to be behind the death directly, but he may be tied to it somehow. After that, she'd report back to Kinley even if she had to show up to meet him empty handed.

Chapter Fourteen
Sleepy Runner

THE LIBRARIAN TORE through the stacks as if she had been waiting for this moment, for the day someone asked about this subject she had been sitting on for quite some time. Kat had tried to leave several times, but the woman kept adding more books and bringing up more details. Her eyes were filled with a fiery passion like Aunt Dot's home had been the subject of her dissertation.

Dante had told her a few stories about the property her aunt's house sat atop, but Kat wanted the true history. Ghost stories were great for campfires, but the reality didn't always match the legends. From what she learned before even leaving the library, this might be one of the few times where that was wrong.

If automatic writing was happening in the house, there had to be a source for the activity. A spirit was the likely choice. Everyone Kat had talked to at length was already under the impression the house was haunted. Plus, she'd never experienced any form of psychic ability in her past. The only other explanation she'd come up with is she was slowly going insane and happened to be doing some lucky guessing along the way. It seemed more likely than a haunted house depending on the day and her mood at the time.

Aunt Dot benefited from this mystical entity. Whoever the spirit was, it had been in the house since before her aunt's death. Kat wanted more than anything for her aunt to be there too. She longed for a message from her, something she'd recognize in an instant was her aunt, but if it hadn't happened yet, Kat was doubtful it ever would.

The most interesting material the library had to share was something Dante never mentioned. At one time, there were tunnels under her aunt's house. They led from the cove beneath the cliffs into the town. Every book she brought home with her had a different account of how widespread these tunnels were and where they reached. The librarian warned her no one really knew for sure. It was a piece of history which had been lost, and there was not enough money in the budget or interest on the council to find out.

She brought the books to the sunroom at the back of the house with a tall glass of wine and the bottle on standby. It wasn't technically a sunroom, but there were enough windows on the porch for Kat to feel validated in calling it such. The view of the trees leading to the cliffs was perfect for her reading.

These tunnels were used during the Civil War, but there were arguments as to how. Most sources claimed the tunnels allowed the safe movement of supplies in the event of an attack. Others felt it was a way to transport prisoners of war without being seen by the locals since many of the prisoners had relation in Fogpoint. Some of these prisoners were reported to have tried to escape. They were killed in the tunnels by the soldiers who captured them.

After the war, they were pretty much abandoned. The military used them for as long as the base remained operational. This was a passage Kat read several times. *'Fogpoint once boasted a military base.'* Surely it was something all the townies were aware of, but it was news to her.

The tunnels were closed to the public in the early twentieth century. They had been deemed too dangerous. Up until that time, they were still in use by many in the town for various reasons. Some took shortcuts in them or snuck around to places where they weren't supposed to be. Children ran through like it was a giant maze.

Many people lost their lives in the tunnels. There were fights which turned deadly, but there wasn't much in the books about why the fighting occurred. Some people tripped, fell, and had injuries too severe to survive. Others got lost and died of thirst.

Multiple things happened at once to encourage the closing of the tunnels. The body of a young child who had been missing for days was discovered below ground not far from his home. The military base announced its closing, and the country was on the eve of prohibition. The tunnels were certainly at risk of being used for rum running.

Before the military base completely moved their operations elsewhere, they closed in all the entrances. Two books had conflicting documentation of how it was done. Both agreed contained explosions were used to close them off, but one maintained the tunnels were also filled in with dirt. Everything she read claimed some entrances were missed, and the tunnels could still be accessed today.

She set the books aside and poured another glass, sipping it while staring at the trees. The answer might be in the tunnels, but there was something far more intriguing. This property had a cell during the Civil War Era; a cell or dungeon, or some other horrid place to stay while awaiting trial. Prisoners were kept here until a fire broke out. All six of the men who were facing charges perished. No one attempted to release them because it was too dangerous between the flames and what they believed the capabilities of the prisoners to be. The fire was left to burn because taming it was a waste of valuable resources.

It was worth examining further, but the books she had only mentioned the tragedy. She'd have to do a lot more digging to verify the details and determine the exact location of where it occurred. It wasn't something she could do tonight.

By her third glass, Kat was feeling rather antsy. She felt like the answers were right in front of her if she only knew where to look. There was a logical explanation behind everything. If it turned out to be a haunting, there had to be a reason for it too. There were ways to banish spirits if one believed in that sort of nonsense. While she didn't know what to believe anymore, she was certain she could find someone to burn some sage or recite a chant once she identified her unwelcome visitors.

According to the roughly drawn map on one of the pages, the tunnels went directly under this property to the cove. The books varied on the information concerning the closures of the entrances, but most of the sources said the entrance from the cove was still open. If it was, she had an overwhelming urge to explore it if she could find it.

Maybe the curiosity was getting to her. There was something going on in this house. She could understand it better if she knew the cause of it. Maybe it was adventure lust. Her life had already been flipped upside down. She was in Fogpoint for a year, met someone new. For as much as she learned about her family, there was so much she still needed to figure out. There was the new job in a position she never expected to find herself in a million years. Maybe it was the three glasses of wine which were hitting just right telling her to do it. Whatever it was, something motivated her enough to go look for the tunnels herself.

The flashlights were in the kitchen and she picked up the first one her fingers touched, turning it on and off to test the batteries. Still in her nightgown, she slipped on a pair of sneakers. *'Go put some socks on, Katrina!'* She could hear her mother yelling at her. *'You know better than to wear tennis shoes without socks.'* Kat walked outside defiantly ignoring her mother scolding her from beyond the grave.

She walked to the edge of the yard and began making her way through the trees from memory. It's funny how the brain picks and chooses what to forget. She couldn't remember her high school locker combination, the one she used for all four years. She couldn't remember what she was wearing when she held her mom's hand as she died from cancer, but she could remember the exact outfit she had on the day her dad got into that fatal car accident. The outfit had hung in her closet until she packed it away in storage for the move. It hadn't been worn since that day. She considered it bad luck, but she also couldn't bear the thought of parting with it.

Yet, she remembered vividly the layout of the trees and could probably make her way to the cove in the dark without the aid of the flashlight by sensing the path with her heart.

Aunt Dot had taken her so many times as a child. She hadn't walked this path for twenty years since returning to Fogpoint, but it stuck out in her mind like it was yesterday. It wasn't the time to test her memory at this hour, and with the amount of wine she had consumed, so she scanned the ground ahead of her with the flashlight as she walked.

They'd walk a safe distance from the edge from one side to the other and back, staring into the blue beyond. Her aunt would always stop and gaze into the cove wistfully, dreaming of days gone by, reliving memories with people no longer around, something Kat hadn't been old enough at the time to recognize. Near the center was a pair of wooden stumps cut down close to the ground, but the gentle eroding of time had them reappearing from the dirt. If you weren't careful, it would be easy to trip over it.

When she asked Aunt Dot about it, she explained there used to be a memorial bench at the top of the cliff. People would use it to sit a spell and remember loved ones lost. Kat had been too young to understand what she meant back then, but now, she could appreciate how having a place to sit while you sink into your sorrow might encourage behaviors best not supported.

The toe of her shoe caught on an exposed root, and she stumbled into a tree, hitting it hard with her left arm. The shoe stayed behind her caught on the root suspended upright on its toe. She retrieved it and squatted down taking the time to tie both of them. The wine hadn't prevented her from tying them before she wandered out of the house. It was because it felt weird wearing sneakers without socks. Instead of acknowledging her mom had been right, her teenage attitude returned with force, declaring she knew what she was doing.

Kat stood up and rubbed her arm where the tree had caught her. It stung, was probably scratched, and there would be a mark in the morning. She was close to the cove, and she slowed her pace after her near fall. In the wrong place, a trip like that meant a long fall into the water where the jagged rocks awaited your arrival. She didn't want to join the property's ghostly legends.

A cool gentle breeze reached her from the water ahead. Her nightgown flew behind her, pasting the front of it to her legs. *'Imagine if something happened to me out here. My ghost would forever be dressed in a nightgown and tennis shoes. A hundred years from now, anyone who saw me would rack their brain trying to figure out the story of the sleepy ghost in running shoes.'* Kat giggled uncontrollably picturing the scene. That was the wine talking.

She reached the cove and was spellbound by the moonlight shimmering over the dark blue of the water. The posts of the bench weren't sticking out of the ground any longer. She searched for them with the light and felt with her foot wanting to mark their place to avoid tripping. They had either been removed or rotted away on their own.

Turning her attention back to the cove, she swayed with the gentle rippling of the water. It was so beautiful and serene out here. She broke herself from the trance and shined her light around the cove on the right side. The beam didn't reach far over the edge. It was silly of her to think she could see anything this late.

A noise behind her startled her, and she spun around quickly, hoping to find nothing more than a rabbit had followed her. Between her sudden movement and not so sober disposition, she lost her balance. Her arms flailed through the air, and the flashlight dropped from her hand. It hit the sides of the cove, breaking apart, before making a small plop in the water below.

Kat felt her body falling backward, and there was nothing around her to grab to prevent herself from toppling over the edge. She closed her eyes and gave in to it, accepting the sleepy runner as her ghostly moniker.

Mere seconds passed, but in her mind's eye, Kat saw everything replay. Her earliest childhood memories when she suffered from night terrors and would wake in a panic, unable to be consoled by her own parents. The summer visits to Aunt Dot's which seemed to last an eternity, and every day was an adventure. The years after her dad died and when she believed her aunt was gone too.

She didn't realize until the moment of her inevitable death how lonely she had been. There were plenty of friends around, but she had taken on a new role of caring for her mom. She was a comfort during her mom's grief and helped more at home while her mom worked two jobs to raise her. Then she cared for her during her mom's initial cancer diagnosis and subsequent reoccurrences. There was no time for maintaining friendships or enjoying her childhood. It was something which never occurred to her before her life was seconds from over.

Another image flashed behind her eyes several times. It was a woman she didn't recognize, but her face stirred feelings of warmth. Whoever she was had been important to Kat, and the trees in the background suggested she met her in Fogpoint. This woman's face and struggling to identify her was likely to be Kat's last thoughts before dying.

A pair of hands grabbed her, pulling her forward. Her eyes remained closed for several seconds. Her body adjusted to being upright once more. She was not alone. When her eyelids fluttered open, her savior was standing directly in front of her. "What are *you* doing here?" she asked.

Chapter Fifteen
The Tunnel

"YOU'RE WELCOME," FRANK said, letting go of her arms.

Kat's hand instinctively pressed against her chest. The feeling of her rapidly beating heart drumming against it was a reminder of how close she had been to the edge of both the cliff and her end. The reality of the situation slowly draped over her like the fog rolling in from the water, clouding her in a gray and desolate veil. Her breathing increased in long, gasping intakes of air which left her more winded after each one. Mere seconds before she had accepted her fate, and it was all sinking in at once.

"Shh," Frank whispered. He took her free hand and led her away from the cove. "It's over now. You're safe."

They walked down a path which ran north of her aunt's property to a side road where his car was parked. Frank gave her a ride back to the house. They made their way in silence. Even Fogpoint treated them with reverence. The streets were empty. There was no movement while the town slept around them as if they knew the two of them had almost faced tragedy and needed time to recover.

When he pulled into the driveway leading up to the Victorian house Kat was barely becoming acquainted with calling home, Frank said, "I haven't been out to the cove for a while now, but something insisted I go there tonight. Now, I know why I was drawn there." He put the car in park and waited.

"Why were you there?" Kat asked.

He clenched his jaw. Kat let it drop realizing it was a subject he didn't want to discuss. She unbuckled her seatbelt and put her hand on the door handle when he began to speak.

"I go there sometimes to clear my head. Talk to my parents."

"Your parents?" Kat wondered out loud.

"Yes. Years ago, it's where my mother..." His voice trailed off.

"Oh, I'm so sorry," Kat told him. She felt like a heel, but she couldn't have known.

Frank shook his head. "She would go there after my father died and sit on the bench for hours at a time, staring off at the water."

"Did your father...?" Kat began.

"No," Frank said. "He was crossing the street and hit by a drunk driver two days after retiring from the force. They had big retirement plans which included a lot of traveling and were looking forward to beginning the next chapter of their life together. As soon as the time rolled around for them, he was gone."

"They loved the water and spent all their free time on it. That's why she went out there. One night the grief was too much, and she decided to join him."

Kat wasn't sure what to say. She wanted to tell him he didn't have to continue if he didn't want to, but she felt like maybe it was something he needed to get off his mind. He was out at the cove, out where his mom lost herself to grief, and it might be good for him to talk about it even if she didn't have the right words to console him.

"Because of that I feel connected to them both on the cliffs. Sometimes when I could really use their advice, I go out there to talk to them in hopes they hear me."

The eerie quiet in the car rattled her more than her near death experience at the cove. Kat wanted to say something, but everything coming to mind didn't seem to be enough. It felt weak and insincere.

"That's why the bench is gone," he added.

Her eyes widened to hear him mention it. She had just been wondering what happened to it not long before he saved her. "It was removed afterward?" she asked.

Frank chuckled, and it was good to see him smile after the weight of what he shared even if she didn't understand why.

"I wouldn't say removed exactly," he grinned. "I went out there with a sledgehammer and made sure nobody else would have a place for their demons to overtake them."

Frank let out an intense sigh as if unburdening himself from the heavy memories. "What were you doing out there? You clearly weren't dressed for the late night walk."

There was a slight flush to her cheeks. For a moment, she'd forgotten about the nightgown she was wearing. She felt childish to admit she was chasing ghost stories and local legends, but he had leveled with her completely. It would be rude to shy away from the truth. "Well," she drew in a breath, staring at her porch. "I heard there used to be a tunnel running under this property to the cove, and I wanted to find the entrance."

From the corner of her eye, she saw a soft smile form on his lips. Frank opened his mouth to say something, but a grin broke on his face. He looked out the window and covered his mouth with his hand.

"Go ahead and laugh," she said with a mix of defeat and humor. "Believe me. I know how funny it sounds."

He took a deep breath and twisted his lips into weird expressions, stretching out the muscles working hard to keep the smirk locked in place. "It's not that," he said. "It's just," he glanced at her. "You're not exactly dressed for underground exploration."

Kat's eyes twinkled, reflecting the light coming from the porch. The corner of her lip turned up, and Frank followed her lead, chuckling at first. The giggling grew and was contagious. Within seconds, they were both laughing until tears leaked from their eyes, and Frank gripped his side, consoling the sharp pain stabbing at him.

"Ah, man," he said, exhaling slowly to regain composure. He wiped his eye with one hand and gripped the steering wheel with the other. "Besides, the tunnel doesn't lead out there. It's a ways to the north."

"Really?" Kat was mildly disappointed. The intrigue of having a secret tunnel in her backyard provided the most amusement she'd had since arriving to this dated tourist town.

"We passed it, actually," he said, nodding at his window in the direction where they'd left the cove. "It would've been too dark to see anything had I pointed it out. Plus it's covered with a grate."

Kat sat upright at attention, craning to see out his window like she could somehow find it through the woods and the darkness. "Just over there?" she asked, pointing in the direction of his gaze.

"That's right," he said without looking to see where she indicated. "I'm not doing anything tomorrow. I can show you if you like, but there's not much to see."

"That'd be great," she said eagerly.

Frank chuckled. "Alright, then. I'll see you in the morning. Say nine? But I meant it when I said it's not much."

"Thank you," she said, still ignoring his warnings. She didn't expect to find a neon sign flashing, "Ghosts This Way." It would be a visual to put to her imaginings. That's all she wanted.

Kat floated into the house happy to have a tour guide showing her the tunnel entrance. She thought she'd have a hard time falling asleep between her near death experience and excitement for the morning, but the wine she'd been drinking earlier had other plans. She was out almost as soon as her head hit the pillow. It knocked her out and kept her out too.

When she opened her eyes again, the clock on her nightstand read 8:47. For a brief second, she basked in the morning light drifting in through the sheer curtain panels on the windows. Then the events of the night before came flooding back, and she shot up with a gasp. Frank would be there at nine sharp, and she was still in bed.

It was the quickest she'd ever readied herself. She threw on clothes, brushed her hair, and touched up yesterday's makeup. There was no time for a shower. Everything she did had to be multitasked. She slipped on her shoes while pulling a shirt over her head. There was a toothbrush hanging precariously from her mouth while she tied the laces on her sneakers. As soon as she was ready, she ran the stairs and made it to the bottom just as the doorbell chimed.

Taking two deep breaths, trying not to have it appear as though she ran which is what she did, she opened the door and greeted Frank with a warm smile. "Good morning! Right on time as always."

"Ready?"

Kat joined him on the porch while Frank asked if she wanted to drive over near where he parked last night. There'd be less of a walk. They could always cut through the woods behind the house if she'd rather.

"Let's walk," she said. "It's a beautiful morning." Letting him lead her across the property meant she could find it again on her easily.

Frank nodded and grinned slowly. "I had a feeling you'd say that." He looked down at his feet.

She followed his gaze and saw the tennis shoes peeking out from under his slacks. It was his day off, but he still wore a suit.

"What have you learned about the property?" Frank asked, leading her off the porch and across the lawn.

"I've mostly been reading about the tunnels," Kat admitted.

"I see." He scowled, and it made her think he disapproved.

"There was a little bit about a fire too."

Frank side eyed her. "The prisoners from the war between the states?"

Kat nodded.

"Sad business. The effects of it still resonate through the

town if you know what you're listening for and where to listen."

He continued to walk and Kat fell into stride a couple paces behind him on his left. Nothing else was added. He had to know why she was doing the research, but he didn't contribute his own theories about the house.

It couldn't be a natural ability. For one thing, she didn't necessarily believe in mediums, and she certainly wasn't one either way. The idea it was familial spirits sticking around had crossed her mind, but she ruled that out too. Kat believed her Aunt Dot's parents were the ones who purchased the house which meant there wouldn't be any spirits before them hanging around. Aunt Dot's mom had helped the police force in her time which meant the ghosts, if that's what was really going on, had to already be there.

Frank slowed his pace and looked around, trying to get his bearings. "Right over here," he said, cutting through the trees.

Kat's mind had been elsewhere for almost the entire walk. She was surprised to see how far they had gone.

She didn't see it until Frank was on top of it. There was a large metal grate on the ground covering the entrance. It was less exciting than the wine led her to believe last night. "This is it?" she mumbled out loud.

His familiar chuckle had become quite comforting to her. While Frank was an elder, a colleague, even a boss to her, his laugh was fast becoming a dear friend. "Like I said, not much to see."

There wasn't anything to look at except maybe two foot of a hole, and that was being generous. Since it was a bright, sunny morning, she hadn't thought to bring a flashlight. Using her cell phone, she shined a light inside, but it didn't help to illuminate much more.

"It goes down at an angle a ways then opens up. An average height man could stand without stooping as he walked," Frank explained.

Kat was immensely disappointed and stared at the grate. There hadn't been any real expectations. She didn't think she'd find a pile of bones or anything like that. She never gave much thought to what she would see, but she had hoped the tunnel was something she could climb inside to explore more thoroughly. This grate wasn't going to budge even with help, and she was fairly sure Frank wouldn't go that far anyway.

"How many do you think lost their life in the tunnels?" she asked, not taking her eyes off the opening in the ground.

Frank scratched the back of his head and squinted in the sun. "Not as many as the stories want you to think, but there were a few."

He extended his arm, motioning toward the way back and waited to see if she was ready.

Kat spun around and began to walk.

"If you're looking for ghosts, the prisoners are a better bet than the tunnels."

Her mood perked up. "Do you know anything about that? Where was the cell or whatever they were held in located?"

Frank chewed the inside of his cheek. "It was a cell. There had been a jail on this property. Back then, the cove provided added security. No one would come from or run to the cliffs."

Things were definitely looking better. "Do you know where it was?"

His eyes twinkled, and his lips curled into a grin. "Well, as I understand it, that house you live in was built over top of it.

Or pretty close to the original location at least."

Kat stopped in her tracks. One thing all ghost stories had in common was location. If her house was built over the site of a fiery grave, a nonbeliever like herself would be likely to accept such a farfetched explanation as a haunting for the weird occurrences.

"Before you go digging up the history of it and talking to those soldiers by name, I think there's something else worth checking out."

"Something more likely to be the source than the death of six prisoners?" This was hard to believe. There was nothing else in the books she had been reading.

"Yeah," Frank said slowly. The house was coming into view already, and he was studying the windows like he expected to see a familiar face peering back at him. "The Harbor Witch."

The words came from his mouth so effortlessly. "Harbor witch?"

"You went to the library here in town?"

"Yeah," Kat said.

Frank sighed and stopped near the porch. "That librarian is an expert on Fogpoint's history, believes every ghost tale ever told about this place, but refuses to give any stock to witches."

Kat happened to agree with the sentiment. Ghosts were hard enough to wrap her head around, but witches were too much for her.

"I think I have a few things," he went on. "Books. Maybe a few articles I've saved over the years. If you'd like, I can bring them to you."

"Sure," Kat said. Feeling like her response was a little lackluster, she added, "Yes, I'd like that. Thank you."

"Alright. I can't guarantee it'll be real soon. Might take me some time to find them."

It was Kat's turn to chuckle. With Frank's organizational skills, she wouldn't be surprised if he had to do a full scale investigation to find anything. "Whenever is fine," she told him. "No rush."

Chapter Sixteen
The Old Barn

DANTE'S SECOND DATE plans, third if you count the surprise ice cream visit, consisted of a picnic hike which Kat welcomed whole heartedly. She wasn't the adventurous type, and her outdoors experience was limited. Other than trips to the ocean with Aunt Dot and a week camping experience in the third grade, she preferred to stay within city limits. The week she spent that summer had been a nightmare. Between the bugs and the dirt, she counted off the hours until her mom returned to get her.

The seafood restaurant he picked for their first date had to be worse than nature in her mind. She ordered chicken, but she couldn't taste it. The entire place was smothered in the scent of shrimp, fish and a variety of other water inhabitants. Her senses were assaulted. Every bite she took tasted the way the restaurant smelled. Anything had to be better than that.

Kat didn't bring a good pair of hiking shoes with her. She didn't own a pair to bring. The best she had were her sneakers, but she spent far too long cleaning them after her nighttime exploration to the cove. The thought of doing it again, only with the shoes in imaginably worse shape, wasn't appealing.

For days she put off buying a new pair. Ever since the garage sale, she had avoided going anywhere public unless she was with someone with the exception of work. She already felt eyes following her all the time, but now, she was convinced she was trapped in a movie she once saw where a girl was outcast because of her family's unusual history. It wouldn't surprise her if the townsfolk began pointing and chanting, "Witch! Witch! Witch!"

The morning of the hike she found herself staring at the closet with the age old dilemma of not having a thing to wear. *'I could cancel,'* she thought to herself. The notice was short, but it wouldn't be the first time she backed out on a date at the last second. The difference was she actually wanted to go on this one.

'Just wear the sneakers,' she scolded herself. *'If you don't want to clean them up, buy a new pair later.'* If shopping wasn't the problem, she wouldn't be in this position in the first place.

She was sitting on the edge of her aunt's bed, and something kept drawing her eye to the wardrobe. For lack of a better idea, she went to it and threw open the doors. Her aunt's shoes were arranged neatly on shelves at the bottom with the exception of one pair. There was a brand new looking pair of lavender accented sneakers laying at the bottom.

Kat closed the doors and walked over to the bed. There was no way she was wearing those to go hiking, but they'd likely become her new pair of shoes when they returned.

It took longer than it should, and she considered canceling over a dozen times before she made her way downstairs to wait for him. She wouldn't have to wait long. Kat had no sooner filled two large sports bottles, one with water and the other with iced tea, when Dante pulled into the driveway. She took a deep breath and cracked her neck, wondering one last time if it was too late to cancel.

"Hi!" She plastered a smile on her face when she answered the door.

He took her backpack while she locked the door and led her to the car. The drive out of town was peaceful, and she realized while she had been focused on avoiding the town, primarily the people who lived there, she forgot about the vast nature surrounding her. Fogpoint's only asset wasn't the ocean. There was plenty she could be doing to occupy her time over this year, and she hadn't seen the woods since she drove through them when she arrived.

Dante navigated the country easily like she'd expect someone from the area to do. Not long into the drive, distracted by their small talk, she became lost. A couple turns escaped her hawk eyed attention, and she really didn't know which direction they were heading any longer.

The trees settled into a blanket of pine, and it seemed familiar in a comforting way. *'Of course, I've probably been out this way before when I was a child. Aunt Dot and I went on many adventures outside of town as well as within the city limits.'*

"The road is going to get rough, but trust me," Dante chuckled. "It turns out onto another paved road which leads to the nature preserves entrance."

Kat smiled politely and gazed out the window, watching the barbed wire fence speed past. Up ahead was an old building in the field. It probably served its purpose well decades ago, but it had fallen into a terrible state of deterioration. On the side of it was a faded patchwork star. Its colors barely visible after years of wear from the elements.

Kat bolted upright and peered out the window with her mouth hung open.

"What?" Dante asked.

"I know this place."

"What?" he asked again.

"Aunt Dot had a painting in her kitchen nook. This is the building in the painting, only it was in much better condition."

Kat felt the car slowing down, and she was appreciative. They were almost passing it, and the closer she got to it the more confident she became this was the exact location where the woman walked holding the hand of the young child in the painting.

"I don't know anything about a painting, but it doesn't surprise me."

She looked at him blankly not sure what he meant.

"I mean," he side eyed her. "This property does belong to your Aunt's daughter."

That was news to her. Kat had never been told the painting was inspired by family land. Or rather, if she had been told, she was too young to remember it. "You mean it used to be her property." She propped her elbow on the door next to the window and rested her head in her hand.

"No," Dante said. The car rolled to a stop, and he put it in park next to the old barn. "She still lives here last I heard."

Aunt Dot's daughter had died. She had one granddaughter who passed away in her late teens. There was no surviving family. As much as it broke Kat's heart, it was the truth. "You must be thinking of someone else," she said quietly.

"Maggie?" he asked. "Oh, what is her name now? Marshall. Maggie Marshall, but it was Edmonton until she remarried."

Kat tried to speak many times, but couldn't find the words. She had met Maggie many times, and she had always been introduced as Aunt Dot's friend, nothing more. Besides, if her daughter was still alive, why did Aunt Dot leave everything to her? Of course, there had to be a secondary option. If Kat didn't finish out the year, the estate had to go to someone else. *'I bet Maggie is patiently waiting for me to skip town.'*

"Take me there," she said in a voice which sounded a little too demanding. "Please," she added, not trying to be rude.

"Where?"

"Maggie's house," she pointed out the window.

Dante started driving again. He didn't say anything until he turned onto the paved road. "Alright," he said. "We'll go to Maggie's."

He had to make a couple more turns to find the front side of the property, but soon they were driving down a long gravel lane to a white farmhouse almost in need of a makeover as badly as the old barn. It looked abandoned, and Kat considered telling Dante she had changed her mind. If Aunt Dot's daughter was still alive and living in this house, she had to be close to seventy years old, maybe older. It was wrong for her to be sitting on a small fortune less than a year away while Maggie received nothing.

The car came to a stop, and Kat stared at the house through the window. There was no movement, no sound. Dante had to be wrong. There were no vehicles or any other signs someone lived there. Aside from the grass having been mowed relatively recently, it looked like the house had been empty for years. A caretaker could be keeping up on the property just as easily as a resident.

He turned off the car, and said, "Let's go." He opened his car door and waited.

Slowly, Kat unbuckled and opened her door as well. They walked up the steps on the front porch together, and Kat couldn't remember being this nervous except for when she was waiting on Dante to arrive for their first date.

Dante stood by her side, but he waited for her to knock. She pulled back the squeaky screen door which was covered in decades of dirt and grime and used the knocker to sound out three loud raps. The door banged shut when she let it go, and Kat cringed, hating the racket she was making. If Maggie was alive and lived here, the noise from the porch might be alarming.

Nothing.

"Does the doorbell work?" he asked.

Kat hadn't noticed the small button to the left of the door frame, but she pushed it. Neither of them heard it chime which wasn't a surefire indicator it was out of order.

She curled a lock of hair around her finger and stared at a warped board a few feet behind Dante. *How long is the right amount of time to wait?'*

As if he read her mind, he said, "Once more. Then we leave." He pulled the screen door open and pounded the knocker into the wood much harder than her first attempt.

They waited a couple more minutes, and then Dante swung his hands together and clasped them. It was all the sign Kat needed, and she quickly walked back down the steps. She couldn't get to his car fast enough. He followed at her heels.

Both were eager to leave. Kat was in a hurry to get to the car, and Dante worried if she were alright. They left so fast without a thought about what if someone was home. Neither of them noticed the curtain move, or that it stayed slightly pulled back until the car was far down the drive. Someone was watching them leave.

"You alright?" he asked, getting in the car after her.

"Yeah. Why?"

"You practically ran to the car."

Kat shrugged one shoulder and smiled softly. "Just ready to get back on schedule," she half lied.

He steered the car down the driveway, telling her, "It's okay, you know."

She wasn't sure what he meant.

"You just learned you have family here. You must be a mess of emotions."

Actually, Kat hadn't thought about it that way. This was Aunt Dot's daughter, yes. The daughter of her *great* aunt which meant Maggie was her aunt. She hadn't made the familial connection to herself yet, only to Aunt Dot.

Dante was right. She wasn't as alone as she thought she was, as she had been for all these years. There was still someone, for however long she had left, who could help her uncover her roots and possibly answer some of these questions which keep piling up all around her.

"I don't know. I met her a few times, but she was always introduce as Aunt Dot's friend. I didn't know there was other family."

"Well," Dante glanced at her. "It was a long time ago."

"No," Kat objected.

"It was. Maybe you don't remember everything."

"No," she insisted. "It was constant. This is my friend. That's what Aunt Dot would say. My friend did this. My friend gave me that. Even when Maggie wasn't there, she was my aunt's friend. I never addressed her as Aunt Maggie. Not once."

"Maybe she didn't know you were in town," Dante went on. "I'm sure there's a reasonable explanation why she hasn't contacted you yet."

'That's right,' Kat thought. *I didn't think she was alive, but she certainly knew about me. It's the inheritance. That's what's keeping her away. She's angry.*

In a flash, her daydreams about having a family again exploded and faded away into darkness. All she had to do was give up one year, and she would be able to have any life she wanted, wherever she wanted.

"I can always bring you back out here at another time," Dante offered. "There's probably a logical explanation why she hasn't stopped by."

"No," she said softly. It's not just that Maggie hadn't contacted her. It was because of the inheritance. Nothing can turn family against family faster than money. Maggie wasn't keen on splitting her mom's estate with anyone, especially someone who hadn't been around the last two decades. 'Or worse.' Kat thought. *Maybe Maggie doesn't get anything unless I'm not able to tough it out for a year.*

At the end of the drive, he asked, "What do you want to do?" If you tell me you want to go back home, I'll understand."

It was tempting. Her spirit wasn't in a date mood any longer. She wanted the comfort of her own home, her own bed, and her own pillow. She wanted to go where she could let out everything she was feeling in the form of little drops which would dampen the pillow case leaving mascara stained rings beneath her cheek.

Except she didn't have her own place. She had the Victorian house which had belonged to a woman once dearly loved, but who was now shrouded in mystery. She didn't have her own bed. She only had the one that used to belong to her aunt. The pillows weren't hers either. Everything she had felt like it was borrowed.

"No," she told him. "I think I could use the distraction."

They agreed to skip the hike. The day had already been exhausting for Kat, but they could still enjoy the picnic lunch while they were in the area. She hoped after a little bit of time to process everything she might feel like her old self again and be ready to face a several mile path through nature with Dante at her side.

Dante turned onto the road and headed toward the nature preserve. They passed a pickup driven by an older man. Neither of them paid him much attention. They didn't notice how the truck slowed down as their car approached. The driver sneered out the window, gripping the wheel until long after they disappeared behind him.

Chapter Seventeen
Family Secrets

KAT STARED AT THE EMPTY wall in the kitchen where the painting used to hang. Many things were beginning to click while others were tumbling out of control adding to the chaos around her. Aunt Dot hadn't removed the painting. She was positive it would've been replaced with one of the many others scattered throughout the house anywhere they'd fit if she had. Someone else took it and likely without Aunt Dot's permission.

She had already suspected someone had been in the house between the months when her aunt passed away and when she arrived in Fogpoint. That person didn't break in. There were no signs of a forced entry, no broken windows, busted locks, or damaged door frames. It had to be someone who had been authorized to take care of the property until she arrived, or who at the very least had a key to the house.

If Maggie was still alive, it was easy to think it was her. The barn in the painting was the one on her property which explained her interest in it. Kat would've let her have it if she had asked.

Looking at the blank wall now, remembering the young child in the red overalls, Kat was sure the child was her. She was the inspiration for the child if not the actual subject anyway. The only reason she had ever thought so was because she had owned a similar outfit, but maybe there were more details her younger self remembered than she could recall now. The other woman in the picture must've been Aunt Dot. The woman's back was turned, so it could've been Maggie.

'Nah,' she thought. The woman in the painting had been young. It was clear even from the angle she was poised. *If it was Maggie or Aunt Dot in the painting, then the child wasn't me.*

It could be Maggie's daughter. She had always been told Aunt Dot's granddaughter had died after an illness, and her own daughter passed away not long afterward. *Would they have given me the hand me downs from a child who passed away?*

A shudder went through her spine. There was probably nothing wrong with it, but the thought upset her.

Kat needed to finish the house. The only rooms left were her old bedroom, the basement and the garage. She'd been saving her room for last as a reward for finishing the overwhelming project, but after the feeling of homesickness that came over her when she was out with Dante, she realized she needed the comfort and familiarity of it sooner rather than later.

The bed she slept on as a child still wasn't hers. It was a guest room which had probably housed many visitors over the years. Yet, it was the closest she had to her own bed on the coast.

Before she opened the door to her old room, she gave the spare bedroom she had been working in last one more look to make sure she hadn't forgotten anything. On the bed was the manila envelope she found when she crashed into the wardrobe. She had completely forgotten about it.

She sat on the bed and looked through the paperwork inside the envelope. It was about Jillian, but if the dates on these papers were correct, Maggie's daughter was still alive after Kat was born. According to these documents, she was a ward of the state a couple hours up the coast at the Elmdale Institution. Kat couldn't be sure if Jillian was still there. The dates on the paperwork were over twenty-five years old. The list of diagnosis on the forms in Kat's hand read like an encyclopedia for mental health issues. Among the ones listed were schizophrenia, PTSD, anxiety and hallucinations.

Jillian wasn't the only one in the family with mental health conditions. Aunt Dot seemingly had some of her own. There was one side of her who hoarded and blocked off rooms while another side was meticulously organized as seen in her bedroom. Everything was in its place.

'The downstairs den... Do they still call it that? Study? Library? Whatever the name for the room, it was also neatly put together.' Any document Kat had needed to find was organized in a drawer of the desk, neatly labeled and ready to be found. It confused her why this envelope was stashed on top of the wardrobe in the spare room where she might not ever have found it if she hadn't been a klutz.

Kat gasped when the thought hit her and looked up at the wardrobe. *'It was a spare room. It was possible Maggie stayed here, in this room, at some point.'* She didn't know much about Aunt Dot's daughter who she still had a hard time reconciling with the person she knew as her aunt's friend Maggie. She did know Maggie had remarried after having gone through a nasty divorce.

Looking over the paperwork again, there was only one emergency contact listed and only one parental signature. Maggie had listed herself as *Ms.* Margaret Edmonton indicating she had already split from her first husband at the time Jillian was admitted.

Part of the paperwork was a long detailed list of medication history. It seemed Jillian had gone through several trial treatments before they found the correct combination to help. The list was several years long. The most current document she could find by flipping through was over fifteen years old. There was too much here to go over right now. It would take hours reading through it all.

Kat stared at the hard wood floor. The only person left to ask about this was Maggie, and she wasn't sure how receiving of company she would be. *'I should've left a note when I was there,'* she thought.

"No," she said, getting to her feet. She tucked all the paperwork into the envelope and carried it downstairs with her. For the first time she notice the name, Jillian Edmonton, in the upper right corner of the envelope. "She knows I'm here."

If Maggie hadn't reached out to her yet, then Maggie didn't want to see her. Whether it was because she was upset over the inheritance or some other reason, Kat couldn't be sure.

She looked up Elmdale on her phone while she heated up a quick lunch. It had a reputation for being a long term treatment facility. The right thing to do might be to contribute some of the inheritance to Jillian's care. It had to be expensive keeping up with the bills if Jillian was still there, but she didn't know how to find out without talking to Maggie.

"Ugh," she groaned. "I'll make another trip to the country."

Her food sat on the table, waiting for her, but she had lost her appetite. The day was getting away from her. The laundry list of work she still needed to get done kept growing longer. It felt like the more she cleaned the more work she found hidden in the clutter. She needed to eat, to keep her energy up to do it.

Slowly she nibbled at it trying to put the family puzzle together in her mind. Dot was actually her great aunt, making Maggie her aunt. Jillian would be her cousin. *'Where does my mom fit in? I always thought she was Aunt Dot's much younger sister, but now I have no idea where her branch in the family tree is located.'*

Everything was now pointing to a visit with Maggie. Kat would try again. She couldn't force Maggie to talk to her, but she wasn't going to leave Fogpoint without doing everything she could to try to unravel the mysteries. There'd be no regrets. She was putting her dishes in the sink when a new, more depressing thought hit her. Even though she's learned she still has family, she's still alone. Perhaps more now than before.

She grabbed the envelope and walked down the hall to put it with her notes from the investigation. Detective Kinley had explained she had access to the databases at work. Maybe she could find out more about Maggie and Jillian before she tried again, but she hoped Maggie would speak to her. There was a reason she was told her aunt's daughter and granddaughter had died, and she wanted to know why.

Halfway down the hall there was a knock on the door. Kat wasn't expecting anyone. She tiptoed the rest of the way trying to peek through the windows on the side of the door, but whoever it was stood directly in front of the door, making it impossible to see them without moving closer.

When she was a couple feet away, Dante leaned to the right to peer inside. His sudden movement caused Kat to jump and drop the envelope. The paperwork inside fell partially free. A few papers flew across the floor, but most just laid half in and half out. "Just a minute," she called out, straightening everything again.

One small paper, more like a card on heavier stock, landed under the table in the hallway. It went unnoticed by Kat. The creamy color of it blended well with the flooring, it had landed face down, hiding the writing on it. If she had seen it, she would've insisted Dante take her to Maggie's right away.

Kat picked up everything she could see and gave the hallway a quick scan to see if she missed anything. Once everything was back inside the envelope, she opened the door. "Hey, you," she smiled. "What a nice surprise." The smile on her face was a little forced because she had a lot on her mind, but she was happy to see him. She was always happy to see him.

"You sure?" he asked. "You look a little frazzled. I should've called first."

"No, not at all," she said, stepping back so he could walk inside.

"What do you got there?" he asked, pointing to the envelope.

Kat grabbed the planner laying on the table next to her purse. "Oh, nothing," she lied. She tucked the envelope inside of it as well as she could with the edges sticking out. The name of Dot's granddaughter could be seen on the top, so she opened the planner again to flip it over, not wanting Dante's curiosity to grow larger.

"Doesn't seem like nothing," he said. "What is it? Case notes?"

"Something like that," she lied again. Although, it could be considered documents for a case she was working on, just not an official one. It was the case of her peculiar family she was trying to solve.

Lying to Dante was painful to her. Lying in general was hard enough. She didn't believe she was very good at it. There'd come a time when she would tell Dante the truth about what she discovered. *'Maybe. I am still planning to leave Fogpoint in the spring.'* Dante made everything more confusing.

Kat hadn't heard any talk around town about Jillian. Even Dante didn't mention anything about her history of mental illness the one time they discussed her. Somehow with all the accusations flung at her aunt for being crazy, Jillian was left out of the gossip. Kat wanted to keep it that way.

It was bad enough having the unfound rumors spreading like wildfire. She could only imagine what the townsfolk would say if they found out there was a history of psychiatric care in her family. More than that, she worried what Dante would think. He might not want to be with her anymore if he found out she had bad blood running through her veins.

"Kat!" Dante said loudly. He waved his hand in front of her face.

She looked at him in a daze. "Huh?" she muttered.

"Where did you go just now?" he laughed. "I asked you a question, but you were off in another world."

"I'm sorry," she said. She glanced at the envelope then looked away quickly, mad at herself for drawing even more attention to it. "I just have so much on my mind."

Dante nodded and sighed. "No leads yet, huh?"

It took Kat a minute to remember he thought they were talking about the case. "That's right." She fumbled her words too quickly and took a deep breath hoping it'd help her speak more normally. "I still have a few things to look into, but coming up empty so far."

"And the house isn't helping?"

Kat cut her eyes to the side. It still irritated her. Yes, there was something more to this Victorian house than meets the eye, and she was finally coming around to being able to admit it. She wasn't ready to openly discuss and sprinkle around comments about it so easily. This needed to progress at a slower rate than people seemed willing to allow. "You said you had asked me a question," Kat reminded him. She ignored the crack about the house.

"Yeah," he said. "I was going to call you tonight, but I left work at lunch. Slow day. Thought I'd just stop by and hope you were home."

As much as she enjoyed his company, she hoped he wasn't asking her out on a last minute date for that evening. Half the day had got away from her, and the only thing she had to show for it was adding to the long list of questions she already had about Aunt Dot's family.

"Well, I'm here," she said awkwardly, forcing another smile when he didn't continue.

"The Farmer's Market is back starting tomorrow. Thought I'd see if you'd like to go?"

Kat didn't have much need to shop there. Most of her meals required venting a pouch and microwaving for three to five minutes. She loved to cook, but it seemed a wasted effort if she was the only one eating.

"I'd love to," she told him. Some farmer's markets had more than produce. There might be something that'll catch her eye, and any time spent with Dante was time well spent. *'There you go again. Reel it back!'*

"Great! I'll pick you up at eight then?"

"Sounds good," she told him.

"Well," he said, clapping his hands and rubbing them together. "I better go and let you get back to ... detecting," he finished with a laugh. He leaned over and kissed her cheek before walking to the door. "See you in the morning."

Kat shut the door behind him and shook her head, exhaling deeply in relief. *'He can't find out,'* she told herself. *'For the sake of our relationship, and the sake of Aunt Dot's already tarnished reputation, he can't find out about Jillian.'*

Chapter Eighteen
The Harbor Witch

RESTING NEXT TO HER on the little table beside her chair on the porch was the journal. She was the one who had brought it outside with her, but all of her thoughts had been running away from her that morning. She had forgotten about the journal as easily as she had forgotten Dante was coming over to take her to the farmer's market until she saw his car pull into the drive.

The journal had stayed on the desk in the bedroom since the first morning she attempted to write in it, having someone else's words appear instead. Occasionally she would open it and try again. That's exactly what she did after getting dressed today.

There had been no new messages scrawled inside of it. The house had been silent ever since the second message. Kat tried everything she could think of to get the house to tell her more, to direct her where to look, or better yet, just tell her who did it.

Carrying it down to the kitchen hadn't been something she intended to do. She stared at it while eating her breakfast, wondering why it had followed her. She couldn't escape the feeling the journal didn't want her leaving it behind.

After she ate, she took a cup of coffee onto the porch to clear her head, planning on returning the journal to the bedroom before stepping outside, but the moment she left the kitchen that plan had disappeared too. She adjusted the pillows on her chair and sat down. When she reached for her mug, she saw the journal sitting next to it. *'Oh, well,'* she thought. *'I'll put it back eventually.'*

Then Dante arrived. At first, she thought it was a pleasant surprise. Then she caught fragments of a vague memory of what they were supposed to do today. *'Good thing I'm dressed.'*

He walked up on the porch and leaned down, kissing her on the cheek. "Good morning," he said. "Are you ready?"

"Just about." Kat glanced at her watch. "I'm just finishing my coffee."

He sat down in the chair on the other side of the table and reached for the blank book. Kat quickly put her hand on top of it, holding it in place and hitting her coffee mug in the process. Dante's quick reflexes moved to catch it and right it before it spilled while Kat held firmly onto the journal.

"Sorry," she mumbled, feeling awkward and foolish.

Dante shook his head. "It happens. What's so important about that book you don't want me to see?" He raised an eyebrow and puckered his lips.

Kat's cheeks flushed. "It's nothing like that."

He didn't reach for it again, but he studied the cover closer. The parts not hidden by her hand at least because Kat was unwilling to relax a muscle of her hold. With a puzzled look on his face, he asked, "Is that a journal?"

"No, I don't keep a journal," she scoffed. The words were a regret as soon as she said them. Saying it was a journal might have kept him from acting on his curiosity. That's not to say people don't snoop in others' diaries. It happens all the time, but he wouldn't be so forward to do it in front of her.

Dante looked out across the front lawn. The expression on his face had changed since he arrived from warm and affectionate, to playful, to serious and possibly irritated. "What's the big secret, Kat? I know you're keeping something for me."

"What?" she chuckled nervously.

"Is it notes for the case?"

"No," she replied truthfully. She reprimanded herself again for being so honest. Something like that would have a confidential quality to them preventing Dante from flipping through the pages. Technically, there were case notes in the journal; they just weren't *her* notes.

Dante leaned forward with his elbows on his knees, rubbing his hands together. He turned his head toward her, but didn't look at her. "I can feel you pulling back, Kat. Did I do something? Is it just cold feet? It feels like there's something you're not telling me, something you desperately don't want me to find out."

She was crushed. She had been looking forward to seeing Dante again even if her mind had been in a daze since getting out of bed. Every moment they spent together was the highlight of her day. He was going to be the hardest part of leaving Fogpoint behind. The logical part of her brain insisted she end things with him sooner rather than later, but her heart refused.

"It's nothing," she told him. "Yes, it's supposed to be a journal. It was a gift from Aunt Dot I found in the bedroom with a note to me inside it. My aunt journaled everything, but it was something I never got into."

Kat opened the book from the bottom and started flipping the pages from the back to the front, showing Dante they were blank. She was careful to stop before she got to the pages with automatic writing on them. Then her handwriting appeared, shocking her. It was a quick grocery list she had jotted down. By the looks of it, she hadn't been in Fogpoint long when she made it. Just trash bags and various supplies needed to work on cleaning out the rooms. *That's why I couldn't find my list that day I went to the store,* she smiled.

"Okay, so I did write in it. I made a grocery list."

"What's so secret about that? This is what I mean, Kat. There's so much you close off. If something that unimportant causes you to practically karate chop a coffee mug to keep me from seeing it, I can't help but wonder what else are you hiding?"

The words cut her deeply. It wasn't that she didn't trust Dante. He believed in the spirits lurking in her aunt's house. He would probably find it fascinating, possibly want to try it for himself. It was because he believed in it she was hesitant. Kat was still struggling to accept everything she learned. Her lifelong presets and beliefs in ghosts, the supernatural, and communication from the beyond had been destroyed. It wasn't easy for her to simply announce to anyone ghosts were talking to her by writing in a journal through her own hand. Just rolling those words around in her head embarrassed her. If she told him the truth, he might encourage her to invite so-called psychics to the house, perform séances, and everything else she used to consider nonsense.

'What about after I leave Fogpoint? Everyone here already has a story about Aunt Dot. I'm not going to add to it.'

"It's just that my aunt gave this to me. It was my last gift from her. It's special. I guess I'm not ready to share it with anyone yet."

After several seconds which stretched on for an eternity, Dante nodded his head and leaned back in his chair. He looked at Kat and smiled. "I can appreciate that. I'm sorry. I didn't know."

Several awkward minutes passed, and Kat sat worrying about how to save their morning when Dante did it for her. "Speaking of secrets, what have you learned about the property?"

As much as Kat wasn't in the mood to discuss ghosts in general, the property's history was a better topic than spirit writing in a journal. "Save that thought. Let me put my mug in the sink, and I'll be ready to go."

Kat walked into the house and into the kitchen. She quickly washed out her mug and left it upside down on the dish mat next to the sink to dry. As she did, she stared out the window at the trees in the back of the house, trying to figure out exactly where the so-called witch might have been killed like she'd been doing ever since reading up on her from the armful of sources Detective Kinley gave her.

The location of the old jail was easier to find. *'If that's really where it had been.'* There was an area of the property where the ground was recessed. The shape of it fits the dimensions, or came close, to the jail. It took a full day's digging in the library looking at old documents which couldn't be checked out to find that information.

When she went back outside, Dante was standing near the door. "I was beginning to think you got lost," he laughed. "Thought I might have to organize a search party."

The two left for the farmer's market, and Kat filled him in on what she'd learned about the harbor witch. "Well, the town's people were half right," she began.

"Oh?" he asked. His curiosity was peaked. Kat never spoke kindly about the residents of Fogpoint.

"There was a witch on this property. It just wasn't my aunt." She immediately realized what she had said and what might come of it, but it was too late. In her fear of what might circulate in the town about the ghosts if Dante ever told a soul, she was desperate to find a different topic. It didn't occur to her witch rumors might actually be worse.

"I've been reading up on the harbor witch," she said reluctantly. She knew Dante wouldn't let her drop the subject now if she tried.

Dante chuckled. He took one side glance at Kat and laughed harder. His amusement continued to gain momentum until his cheeks were fiery red, and he was gasping for air between rolls of belly shaking laughter.

Kat was confused. She didn't know if he was reacting to the absurd name, or if he knew but didn't believe the tales. She wasn't sure what was so funny regarding what this town did to that poor woman so long ago.

"I'm sorry," he said, wiping tears from his eyes. "I haven't heard anyone talk about the harbor witch since I was a child. It's an old ghost story about a banshee screaming from the cliffs at night because she's looking for her husband or something like that."

"There's a little bit of truth in most stories that are passed down," Kat told him. *'She's probably screaming because of where she found him.'*

Near as she could tell, Meredith Fletcher was an old woman living on her own. There was nothing extraordinary about her except she was very knowledgeable about herbs and their uses, old fashioned remedies, and natural healing. The era she lived in was filled with outlandish cure all's and doctors were stuck in their ways with their own treatments for various ailments. Some with better results than others. People came to her for help with a sick child or injury. That was already enough to stir up a fuss in the town.

The library had a collection of old letters and other documents from the town's history. It took some convincing, but the librarian helped Kat navigate through them to find what she needed. Many of them mentioned Meredith because the town elders and other prominent residents weren't happy with her. The local doctor at the time was angry his clientele were going elsewhere instead of fully relying on him. It was him, more than anyone, who instigated Meredith's downfall.

There were many in town she refused to do business with for personal reasons. She would rather buy or trade for what she needed from the family who was poor and struggling then take her business to the general store when its owner was doing well financially. Talk about supporting small business before that became a household phrase. Meredith moved to Fogpoint when it was changing from a rural dependent area to a more mainstream town and business center. She was a little stuck in the past with old ways with how she lived.

Most of these letters were filled with one widespread sentiment: Meredith was a woman. That's what most of the commotion over her boiled down to in the end.

"There's no dealing with her without a husband to make the choices in her best interest."

"It's like talking to a child."

"My cousin's backward daughter has more common sense."

Meredith was a strong woman, and the men in town were intimidated by her. It was evident in everything Kat read.

What sealed the deal was her husband's death. Her *second* husband's death. Her first husband died in the arms of his mistress. That was enough for the hoity-toity members of Fogpoint society to turn up their noses at her. Almost all husbands had mistresses, but theirs were well mannered enough not to die in bed with another woman making a scandal out of it.

When her second husband died the same way as her first, the talk in the town took a turn. They had heart attacks. It was clear from what was available for Kat to read about it. The coincidence was unfortunate and slightly amusing to learn now, but not back then.

Of course, both of these women claimed it was the first encounter they'd had with their lover. They accused the men of seducing them and played the victim well.

That's when the more prominent members of society got together to discuss her. It was decided Meredith Fletcher was a witch who cursed her husbands to die if their eye was ever turned by another woman. *'Those women caught far more than a man's eye.'*

The news of the Salem witch trials while decades old had made its way to Fogpoint. Residents were always on the lookout for evidence witchcraft might make its way to them. Meredith was the embodiment of a witch if there ever was one according to them.

She was paraded out into the town's square where she was forced to strip in front of a panel organized to investigate the accusation of witchcraft, made up entirely of her enemies. The entire community came out to watch and were gathered round as she stood exposed to all. There was a mole on her right leg which they determined was the mark of the beast. She was found guilty and sentenced to death.

"Well, she clearly wasn't an actual witch," Dante said. He was picking out a selection of heirloom tomatoes at one of the tables.

"That doesn't mean she wasn't put to death for it."

"Really?" Dante looked at her surprised. "You know this. For fact?"

They walked on and browsed more tables. "Yes," she said, turning to him and lowering her voice. "With what I found at the library, I think I even found the spot where it happened."

Dante grinned at her. "Was she hung? There's no way the tree is still there. I was always told the harbor witch was our very own version of Salem."

"Yes and no," Kat said. She motioned to him to wait. They were coming up on larger groups of people, and she didn't want their conversation to be overheard. It could wait until they were headed back to the house.

It happened in 1789, almost a full century after Salem's notorious fiasco. Meredith had been sentenced to death by hanging. The largest, strongest tree in town was chosen as the ideal candidate to support her weight. There were two actually, sister trees three feet apart. They were convinced witchcraft was isolated to her, but didn't want to contaminate anything by having her held or put to death where other prisoners might meet the same fate.

She was tied to the tree for three days. On the morning of the hanging, the entire town showed up for the festivities. Someone jokingly asked her which one she wanted to die from, but everyone gasped when she answered. Of course, they used the other tree she didn't pick thinking she must've spelled the first somehow.

When the stool was kicked out from underneath her, the branch broke. Her body tumbled to the ground unharmed. People bolted from the hill. Letters from the doctor spoke of treating multiple injuries due to people being trampled on in the melee caused by fear.

It wasn't enough to stop the execution. They used the rope to tie her to the tree and burn her to death. "So, no the tree isn't still there," she said.

Dante pulled into her driveway. "What makes you think you found the spot then?"

"The other tree is still there, and there's more."

He looked at her in disbelief.

"Come," she said, opening the door as soon as he parked. "I'll show you."

They walked to the back of the house, and she led him to the tree she was talking about. It was a hunch. Kat had nothing to go on for the location except it happened in this area.

She led him to a giant oak tree. The trunk was so large no

adult could wrap their arms around it. Two adults with arms widespread couldn't touch each other if they tried by reaching around opposite sides of the tree.

"Wow," Dante muttered impressed. "I've never seen a tree this massive."

That had been Kat's reaction too. This tree had been her favorite as a child. Even then, Aunt Dot had told her it was over three hundred years old.

"Okay," he nodded. "I admit it's possible, but it doesn't guarantee anything."

"Look here," she said, pointing to the ground just north of the tree.

"What about it?"

"This whole area is dead. Nothing grows."

Dante studied it carefully. "Probably gets too much shade."

"I thought that too, but that's not it. The other side of the tree gets the same amount, but it's green and thriving."

She could tell he still wasn't convinced, so she hit him with the pièce de résistance. "See that?" Kat tilted her head back and looked far up the trunk.

"What am I looking for?" he asked.

"The darkened area up there," she said.

"Yeah? What about it?" Immediately afterward, he added, "Oh my! Is that charring?"

"Yep," Kat beamed. "Hauled the ladder out myself two days ago."

He turned to her and said, "I wouldn't say you think you found the spot anymore. This is definitely it."

They walked back to the front of the house to unload Kat's purchases from his car. "You know what would be cool?" he asked. Before she could answer, he went on. "We should get some people out there and do a séance."

'*This is exactly why I didn't want to talk to him about any of this.*'

"I'd rather not draw any more attention than necessary while I'm here. It's something you could do when I leave. It'll take time for the house to sell, and I wouldn't have a problem with you doing it then." She hadn't realized Dante had stopped walking behind her.

"You're still gonna leave?" he asked.

Kat turned back and saw him several feet away looking heartbroken. It tugged at her emotionally. She wanted to comfort him, take back what she'd said, but she had to stay strong. "You've known all along I'm only here for a year to tidy up my aunt's affairs, get things in order."

The inheritance was something she still hadn't shared with him. She had only told him she expected it to take a year to get everything done. He didn't realize it was finite.

"You're cleaning out the house pretty fast with the help of Sampson. At this rate, it won't take anywhere close to that long."

"There's a lot more than just cleaning out the house for me to do." She tried to assure him a little bit.

"I had hoped maybe you'd reconsider, and you'd stay," he said, setting her bags on the porch. Dante walked back to his car and left without another word.

Chapter Nineteen
Cold Indifference

KAT HAD DRIVEN BY THE art studio at least once every day since her brakes were replaced, but she never had the courage to stop. It was a small hole in the wall place, and she'd be completely out of her element there. Her crafty side consisted of watching the cute how to videos then buying something similar ready to go. It would be hard to fake a reason for being there, and she'd probably be the only one in the store which would make it easy for David to figure out who she was and her true purpose for stopping by.

To her surprise, the art studio was far more impressive than the quiet exterior led her to assume. The floor space was divided into two main parts. The front served as a retail area. There was art in multiple forms everywhere. Paintings with hefty price tags, sculptures which stood almost as tall as Kat, as well as smaller pottery décor items. She checked the price of a small vase and balked. It cost more than an entire paycheck from her job back home.

Her eye kept being drawn to the back. There were two open doorways on either side allowing free movement between the rooms. A counter ran the width between the two doors with a register on either end. A young man she recognized from photographs as David stood behind the counter, shuffling through a pile of paperwork.

In the back, she could spy people working at easels. It was hard to say how many were there because every angle produced new faces, and soon it was too difficult to keep track of who she already counted. She inched her way farther into the retail part of the studio concentrating on the artists in the back. As she did, she looked around for anything which may jump out to her as evidence, either to prove David attacked his grandfather or that he didn't.

There was a lot of hand carved wood pieces for sell too. Kat noticed as she neared the back room there was a display of finials for sale all made by local crafters, many carved from driftwood. *'It would be so easy to blend the murder weapon right in with these,'* she thought. There was a picture of the one taken from the scene which had been compared to the head injury Harold sustained. She couldn't remember exactly what it looked like and didn't have a copy of it with her to compare. The one used in the attack was still missing. It would've been easy to slip it in with the rest. It could've been sold to anyone by now.

"May I help you?" David's cheerful voice made her jump.

Kat swung around to face him so fast she almost fell over. He reached out a hand to help her regain her balance. "I'm sorry," she smiled. "I was lost in my thoughts."

"Looking at the finials," he nodded. He stared at her for the longest minute of her life then broke into a smile. "I understand. I expected you to make a visit to the studio sooner than later, and I figured the finials would catch your eye. That's why I left them on display."

"That's why... You left them?" Kat wasn't sure if she heard him correctly.

"Mmm-hmm," he said, picking up one of the more ornate ones. "I know you're working the case with Detective Kinley. And, I know what they believe the murder weapon was. It would make me look guilty if I hid all these," he said, motioning to the rest of the display without taking his eyes off the one he was holding. He set it down and looked at her sternly. "I'm *not* guilty."

'Was there a public announcement made about my involvement in the case I missed?' Kat was frustrated. It was hard enough to do a job she felt inadequate to do without everyone knowing she was playing a game of amateur detective.

The finials did pique her interest, but she never believed he was guilty. The words, "I don't believe it was you," almost left her mouth, but she caught herself in time.

This was her first case. The orientation videos she watched covered sexual harassment and other inappropriate workplace behaviors, and the minimal training she received reiterated the steps to take in following the chain of command on evidence. At no time had she been taught whether or not to discuss her thoughts on the case with suspects. From what she saw in movies and numerous documentaries, she thought it best to keep it to herself.

She forced a smile at David instead. "You know who I am?"

The disgust written on David's face couldn't be missed. He forced the words out through clenched teeth. "Of course I do. Fogpoint has turned into a bustling tourist city, but it's still a small town at heart. Everyone knows who your aunt was, and I'm well aware of why you're paying my shop this visit."

"Well, I won't be long," Kat said sheepishly. "I'm just doing my job." For someone small in stature, he made up for it in intimidation.

"Do it quickly," he snapped.

A commotion from the back of the shop where the studio was located was a welcome interruption to the tension created in the store front. Someone had knocked over a tray table of supplies. Various items clinked and clanged as they bounced on the tiled floor with the shattering accompaniment of glass breaking.

David's attention was drawn to the back. Without seeing his face, Kat could feel his irritation and anger.

He turned to her, and said, "Excuse me."

Kat followed him to the open doorway. The threshold to the studio was like a magical portal which changed his demeanor instantly. He was smiling, and his tone was very light and upbeat, reassuring the young woman who was the cause of the accident.

"It's okay."

"These things happen."

"Don't worry about it."

"I've made my fair share of messes in here too."

On the floor was a large pool of paint. Various colors were mixing together forming a mosaic swirl which was rather beautiful until the cleanup began. All the colors combined together into a brownish mess of liquid causing Kat to turn her head, clearing her mind of what it had begun to look like.

She browsed the wall in the back of the shop where more

paintings by local artists were hung. They were all quite good. Many of them had sold tags hanging from them. As she made her way to the other side of the store front, she peered through the other doorway to the studio. She could see the work of some of the students sitting in front of their easels. It was quite impressive.

David noticed her and approached her. "Is there anything else?"

Without taking her eyes off of one of the works in progress, she said, "There's a lot of raw talent here in Fogpoint."

He followed her gaze and sighed. "Most people have more artistic ability than they give themselves credit. They've never had any training, learned any techniques to bring forth these images on the canvas."

"The art classes you offer look like they do quite well," she said.

The young woman was finishing putting a few things back in place, but heard enough to join the conversation. "There's multiple classes for different stages."

"Yes," David nodded. "This is one of our intermediate classes. The instructor is actually a professor at the state university."

The woman walked toward them taking a jar of brushes to the sink near where Kat stood. Her blonde ponytail swaying back and forth behind her head. As she passed them, she said, "There's an introductory class that's free. You can try it out before you commit."

If looks could kill, David's eyes would have been shooting daggers on the poor woman.

"Thank you," Kat smiled. "I'm tempted."

"It's pretty booked. It's only offered every other week, and they can book up months out at a time."

David was clearly trying to discourage her. It only served to make Kat want to do it more.

"I don't mind waiting," she said sweetly. "I'm going to be in town for a while, and I don't have much better to fill my time."

Several of the students had turned their attention to the conversation disrupting their concentration. David opened his mouth to dissuade her again, if not flat out refuse her, but saw he had an audience. Not wanting to say anything which would sour the listeners' opinion of him or his business, he said, "Alright, let's get you signed up."

Kat followed him into the store front where he went on a computer behind the counter. His face was twisted into a grotesque expression making him look like he was in pain from the search.

"Well, look at that," he said with a smirk. "There was a cancellation for tomorrow at six."

"Perfect," Kat said. "I'll take it." She had a feeling he was playing a trick on her like she'd walk in to the most advanced class his store offered. To her surprise, she was the only student there.

Kat returned to David's business the next evening. Most of the lights in the store front had already been turned off, and the closed sign hung in the door. She wasn't sure of the retail hours in the front part of the shop, and she tried the door thinking it would still be unlocked for those coming to the class. She was wrong.

It was hard to see into the shop because the windows were blocked by displays. She pulled out her phone to look up the store's number when David appeared suddenly on the other side of the glass causing her to gasp and jump back in surprise.

He wore the same sour scowl he exhibited most of the time she spent with him one day earlier. There was a click, and the door opened. "You came," he sounded disappointed.

"Of course," Kat smiled, ignoring her cold welcome. "I'm actually excited about it."

He opened the door wide and stepped to the side, allowing Kat to enter. He locked the door behind her.

Kat was about to ask how the other students were expected to get in when David said, "I'm ready to begin if you are." He nodded toward the back of the store.

She glanced at her watch. It was still a few minutes till six. She had thought she was early, but not early enough if she was the last to arrive. They walked to the back where the lights shown through the one open door to the studio. That must have been the light she saw from the outside. The other doorway had a curtain hanging over it.

The room had been rearranged completely since she last saw it. Instead of a classroom of easels and supplies, it was now beautifully decorated with various pieces of artwork showcased. At the front of the room in a corner taking up a small bit of space were two easels and a tray of supplies. It would only be her and David this evening.

"Like I said, these classes are booked out months at a time, but I was going to be here tonight preparing for the exhibit this weekend. I thought why not?" he explained. "Take a break from the stress and anxiety of the show and go back to my roots."

Kat was unsure how she felt about being the only student.

Her mind illustrated scenarios detailing what might happen, if David was in fact the murderer. It wasn't the smartest idea being alone like this with the suspect when she was investigating the case. She tried pushing the thoughts away because David was not likely capable of such a violent act, but every time she thought she had cleared her mind, she found herself glancing around for items which could be used as weapons against her.

They settled into the introductory class with David showing her a few techniques. He painted a picture side by side with her, instructing her step by step how to create the same image.

"You said something about going back to your roots," Kat remembered. "Did you used to be an art teacher?"

David frowned like the thought of making small talk was unpleasant. "It's one of my degrees," he said. "My dream was always to open a large gallery in a bigger city."

"Oh," Kat nodded. "That sounds interesting."

"Does it?" he snapped.

"Yes, it does," she said defensively. "Although, I kind of thought that's what this was," she said, motioning around her. "A store front and a gallery."

"It is," David said, returning his brush to the jar of water next to his easel and leaning back. He studied his work before giving it a nod, indicating he was happy with it. "This place works well as a gallery," he told her. The tone of his voice didn't agree with his words. "We have to drape the walls for every show. The bills for cleaning the floor are astronomical even though we use drop cloths in most of our classes. Accidents do still happen like you saw yesterday."

'That's why he was so angry,' Kat thought. *'It wasn't the loss of supplies or the mess. It was because he had a showing soon.'* She nodded to show she was listening.

"This place has been kind to me. It pays for itself, and I'm debt free."

'Because you live with your mother,' Kat sneered inside her head.

"But I can't expand anymore here. It's already as big as it's going to get. I want to do more, *be* more. I need to move to someplace larger. It's just going to take a little while longer than I had hoped to get the funds to do so."

Kat placed her brushes in the jar alongside his. She was happy with her painting of the harbor, but it was at best junior high quality.

"Not bad," David said.

It made Kat smile. He was being kind. She hadn't thought he was capable of such a gesture.

"I mean it," he added. "Is it going up for auction? No. But you do have potential."

Kat stared at her painting again. This time she couldn't be sure if he was being honest or if his Jekyll had won out over his Hyde.

"I'm not surprised," he went on. "Artistry runs in your family." He walked across the room, carrying the jar of brushes to the sink as soon as he said those words.

Kat was left wondering what he meant. The painting which had once hung in her Aunt Dot's house of her Aunt Maggie's barn came to mind. Anyone could've painted it, but now she was curious as to who. She wanted to ask David more about what he meant, but talked herself out of it by the time he returned. He didn't seem interested in idle chatter.

She glanced around at some of the art already on display, and asked, "Do you mind?'

David shrugged and muttered, "Like I have a choice."

The comment bothered Kat. Of course, he had a choice. People paid to come to these showings. He certainly didn't have to allow her to browse around for free. If he was going to cast that kind of attitude toward her, then she would take advantage of the situation by getting a sneak peek.

She stood up and began with the pieces displayed closest to her. The room was dotted with nature scenes, many of them views of the water. The first one had been done by David. It was another harbor painting like they had done tonight, only far more detailed. The harbor lights reflecting off the water at night along with the stars. The city lit up in the background. The shadows over the water showed the life living below the waves.

The next one showcased a sailboat gliding past the cove. It was also by David. She continued on one after another with David following closely at her heels. "These are all yours," she noticed.

"Yes." David stood motionless, not revealing a single thought.

"When you said you had a show, I thought... Well I don't know what I thought," she said. "I just assumed it was more local work."

"I have shows like that as well. Sometimes, I've even highlighted different artists from here, but I like to show off my own ability too."

Kat continued on looking through the paintings. "These

are all amazing," she told him.

"Thank you." It was the first words he'd ever spoke to her that weren't dripping with contempt and sounded like he actually meant them.

As he walked through the store to lock up behind her, he said, "May I ask you something."

"Go ahead."

"Which of the paintings was your favorite?"

"The sailboat passing the cove, of course," she said. "But I might be biased."

David nodded. "And your least favorite?"

"The one of the old business district," she answered.

He narrowed his eyes at her. "Why is that?"

Kat shrugged, and said, "I don't know. Just not my taste." It came out like she was questioning it more than stating a preference.

As she walked down the street to where she had parked her car, she thought about how she lied. Her own personal taste had nothing to do with it. Art was something she knew very little about and had never given much thought to what her preferences might be. The painting looked rushed. The brick exterior of the old barber shop running down the alley had been vandalized many times over, but the splattering of paint of the brick to add to the graffiti included in the painting seemed amateurish. Being someone who could barely draw a stick figure, she was not about to critique the owner of an art studio on the quality of his work.

Chapter Twenty
Whodunit

DETECTIVE KINLEY NEVER ceased to amaze her. He was a walking illustration of being an organized mess. He was one of those people who would be lost if someone came around and cleaned his office or, more than likely, his home. It might look like a disaster area, but he knew where everything was located.

Kat sat in his office watching as he pulled every file, every form, every notepad he had jotted a piece of important information on from one pile or another, or a desk drawer. Once he even crossed the room to grab something from his jacket pocket laying over the arm of the couch.

"So, you're sure?" he asked, cracking his neck from side to side.

She nodded while chewing the inside of her cheek and staring at the notepad on his desk. It had the name she had given him written in large letters in the middle of the page. Frank had gone over it again and again with his pen, making the letters bold, jumping out at anyone who saw it. In fact, it looked like he had ripped through the paper in several spots. He had also circled it repeatedly. The lines looped around each other like the designs she made with a Spirograph when she was a child.

When she looked at him, his eyes were narrowed like he was studying her. He raised one eyebrow as if to say he wasn't as confident as she believed herself to be, but he didn't say a word.

Kat straightened up and laid her hands in her lap. "Yes, I'm sure."

He flipped through the various notes on his desk again and sighed. "The house told you this?" he asked.

It bothered her for some reason. She would be the first to admit her background in no way prepared her for the job. Still, the paychecks hit her account every week. When she insisted there wasn't much she could do besides relay any messages that appeared in the journal, Kinley reiterated his confidence in her. "You'll be a natural, just like your aunt," he had told her.

Whether she really believed those words or not wasn't the point. She had done what was asked. The lives, whereabouts, and motives of both brothers, Harold's grandsons, had been scrutinized. She'd made visits to both of them. Twice!

'Could I be wrong about who did it? Certainly. But I really believe I'm right.'

Now that she was here, in Kinley's office, presenting her findings, he was questioning her. Everything written on his face suggested he wasn't convinced. *'But the house? The house he will trust.'* It did more than just bother her; it infuriated her.

"Not in so many words," Kat said. "But yes." The house didn't give her much information at all, but it provided enough.

Kinley took a deep breath and exhaled while stretching his neck from side to side. "I don't think it's enough for a warrant, but I'll see what I can do."

"About that," Kat said. "I have an idea."

He listened intently as she told him her plan. A grin formed on his face as she spoke and grew larger with each detail. "Now, that can be arranged, Miss Thompson," Kinley said. The light in his eyes twinkled.

Kat left the office wondering how she was going to spend her evening. Dante still wasn't speaking to her since she delivered the news Fogpoint was, and would always be, a temporary stop. It'd be easier if she had him for company. She really wanted to be around when her plan played out, but she worried about if she'd just be in the way. Kinley had assured her that wouldn't be the case, but she didn't want to be the reason it all went wrong.

The empty house stared back at her when she walked through the door. All of the downstairs rooms had been restored to their former glory without a trace of the mountains of junk her aunt had hoarded. There was only the basement and the garage left. Then she'd have nothing to do but pass time until her year was over.

The rooms echoed her footsteps as she walked through them. It was strange how the house seemed so much bigger when she was a child running around the downstairs, letting her imagination carry her away. It seemed smaller now with an emptiness so large she couldn't grasp how the house could hold it all inside.

"Well," she said to the empty vase on the hall table, "I guess there's an art show I could attend."

It was advertised as open to the public which meant David couldn't keep her out without risking a scene at his own showing. He dropped several hints during their class together that he'd rather not see her there. Invitations had been sent out to VIP guests and priority entrance would be given to them. The attendee list would be primarily comprised of the VIP's, critiques, and hopefully a media outlets covering the event. It really wasn't the type of show for a novice to understand the full scope. He loved to dig at her lack of ability.

She went upstairs to change into something more formal. It was either this or sitting home by herself all night, and she was growing tired of her own company. It had always made her feel awkward to take in a movie or go out to a restaurant alone. At the gallery, it might be assumed she was still working the case which could wind up being just as awkward. It was a risk she was willing to take because at least then it might be understood why she was there alone.

Almost an hour later, Kat descended the stairs in a red dress even she had to admit looked amazing. She glanced at her watch. The exhibition opened thirty minutes ago, and she wondered how many people were there. The social etiquette for galleries wasn't something she'd ever learned, and she didn't know if it was best to go earlier or not.

She drove down to the business district off the beach, remembering she had heard it mentioned the alley door was the one in use tonight. It opened directly into the backroom of the art studio where David's work was displayed with a few assorted pieces by other local artists.

After having seen it as a classroom, her breath was taken away when she walked in tonight. It was like she had been transported to an entirely different building. Everything was so clean it sparkled. There wasn't a single easel, tray, or even a brush in sight. The art was showcased in a way where it could be viewed from either direction depending on your preference for timeline. If you preferred linear, you could head to the left and follow the works from scenic rustic landscapes as they grew into a bustling harbor and finally the city itself. Beginning on the right would take you on a journey back in time as the layers of progress were stripped away from Fogpoint.

"And," as she heard one guest remark, "if you're non-linear, just jump around the room in any direction you choose." His joke was met with laughter, but a hush fell over his friends when David approached.

'I see I'm not the only one who doesn't think he owns a sense of humor,' she smirked.

Kat grabbed a glass of champagne off a tray offered to her by a waiter and began making her way to the left. She didn't care which order she viewed them, but this side had fewer people standing around discussing art. It was the quickest way to get away from David who she didn't imagine would be too happy to see her here, and she wasn't going to stick around to find out.

Other people were paired off as couples or in small groups praising the work displayed as she made her way through. It was awkward feeling like she was the only one here alone. People gave her curious glances either wondering who she was or questioning the audacity she had to show up at David's exhibit when she was working the case of his grandfather's murder.

A waiter was making his way through the rows of artwork, and she gulped down the champagne in her glass to replace it with another when he got close. The bubbles went straight to her head making her feel fuzzy, and she warned herself not to drink a lot. There was too much she could risk tonight including the drive home if she got carried away.

The painting of the sailboat near the cove was one of the first ones she displayed. It was just as beautiful now as it was when she first saw it after her introductory art class. There was something comforting about it. The way the person on the sailboat was navigating the waters masterfully, not needing anyone's help to make their way. The cove of course reminded her of childhood, of a past which was sometimes painful, but filled with memories to last a lifetime.

She looked around at the others nearby, hoping she could read minds. *'Maybe I could buy it?'* she thought. *'Should I?'*

Kat struggled with figuring out the moral line in this situation. She wasn't a detective assigned to the case, merely a consultant. There had to be rules about fraternizing with suspects, but buying a painting was nowhere near the same thing as jumping into someone's bed. It was possible this could fall into that gray area between right and wrong, but it was just a painting. *'What harm could it do?'*

Taking a step closer, she looked at the small card next to the painting. *'It's called "Night Sailing," and it's... how much?'* Kat sipped down the champagne again a little too easily and stopped halfway through the glass. She continued on, eyeing people sideways, hoping no one saw the embarrassing way she reacted to the price tag listed on the painting. Her eyes had popped, and she was still dragging her lower jaw on the floor.

'Twenty-seven hundred dollars!'

Kat could cover the cost. The majority of the year's allotment to stay in the house was still in her account. That wasn't the point. She couldn't justify spending that much money on one piece of art she'd hang on the wall and forget. The argument of whether or not it was morally wrong for her to purchase it was over. It was now about whether it was right for an unknown artist like David to charge so much for his work.

None of the rest of the paintings jumped out at her. She didn't think any of them would touch her in the way the one of the cove did. That one was close to home, more personal. They were all beautifully done. He was very talented. Some even displayed they were sold by a small red sticker placed on the corner of the name plate for the piece, and she felt embarrassed for asking what they meant.

While studying one of the paintings of the harbor, a man came over, an employee she assumed, and placed one of the stickers on the name plate. "Excuse me," she said to him. "What's that for?"

"This?" he asked, holding up the sheet in his hand.

"Yes."

"It means someone just purchased it."

There was a snicker nearby, but when Kat turned her head, she didn't see who had been laughing. She assumed whoever it was had laughed at her, had found her ignorance funny. She lifted the glass to her lips, then lowered it. The second glass of champagne needed to last until she left. Without the alcohol to ease her nerves, she moved on quickly.

When she made her way around the last bend of the showcase, she came across another painting she recognized. "Graffiti Alley" had been her least favorite when she took a sneak peek after her class, and she liked it even less now. The tag on it read five hundred dollars, and it had already been sold.

"Surprised?" A familiar voice sent a shiver down her spine, and she straightened up.

"About what?" she asked.

David walked directly in front of his painting and folded his arms across his chest. "Are you surprised your least favorite piece was one of the first to sell?"

It was a dig at her lack of art knowledge, but two could play this game. "Not nearly as surprised as I was to see my favorite one has the highest price tag of any of the paintings here."

He glared at her, and she was thankful for the audience it'd draw if he let loose what was on his mind. "I didn't expect to see you tonight," he said.

There were a million comments running through her mind, but she didn't bother with them. "I just didn't feel like spending the night at home," she admitted. "Then I remembered your show, and here I am," she said, adding a truce smile at the end.

The smirk on his face rejected her peace treaty. "I see. What about that man of yours? Hmm? Trouble in paradise?"

Fogpoint really was still a small town at heart regardless of how large it'd grown the way gossip traveled around. "No," she said, not sure if it was a lie. "We're just doing our own thing tonight."

David nodded in agreement, but his eyes sparkled like he didn't believe her. "Well, a man like that is hard to find. It'd take someone special to hold on to him," he said.

'Ouch!'

"Excuse me," and, he was gone. David drifted off calling to someone he recognized. They greeted each other and soon peals of laughter rang out from them.

'Enough of that,' she thought, examining her champagne. Instead of drinking it, she placed it on the nearest waiter's tray and left the studio. It was time to go home and relax.

On the drive home, all she could think about was a luxuriously hot bubble bath to release the tension she was feeling. It was too early yet for an update from Kinley, but she hoped to hear some news before too long. She was feeling thankful she wasn't around for any part of their plan for the evening. There was still a process before the arrest, and she was going to drive herself crazy during the wait. She knew she was right, had to be, but an arrest couldn't be made on her word alone. They needed proof.

She walked into her house with lavender scented visions of bubbles in her head, but didn't make it past the dining room. The five generation family painting stopped her. All of their eyes stared at her, showing their displeasure. Kat slumped into one of the chairs at the end of the table and fiddled with her cell phone. She scrolled through the call history until she found the number she was looking for and tapped it to dial.

It rang twice before there was an answer. "Hello."

"Dante? Are you busy?" she asked.

Chapter Twenty-One
Good in... The Kitchen

KAT WAS SURPRISED DANTE was giving her a second chance. She hadn't heard a word from him since the night it slipped out she wasn't planning on staying in Fogpoint permanently. They'd only had a couple official dates, but they typically texted each other on and off all day long. He hadn't responded to any of her messages since that night. Shoot, she was surprised he answered when she called.

They weren't going out tonight. Dante was cooking for her. She sat at the table in his kitchen watching him expertly dice vegetables. This was something she could get used to. With her culinary skills, she had always known she'd have to marry someone who knew his way around a kitchen.

'Whoa,' she giggled. *'Married? Slow down there, cowgirl.'*

"What's so funny?" Dante asked.

"Nothing," she shook her head and waved him off. When she glanced at him, he raised one eyebrow to question her again. "I was just thinking how it was nice to have someone cook for me. It's a nice change."

He paused and thought about it. "You're right. It would be

a nice change to have someone cook for me," he said, giving her a challenging look.

"Well, I don't know who that's going to be. Trust me. You don't want me anywhere near the kitchen."

They both laughed, and it felt so nice. It was like nothing had happened. They eased back into each other's company so effortlessly.

Kat grew quiet after that thinking about going home and how much she would miss Dante. She hadn't known him long, but she could tell he was different than anyone she'd ever met. All of her ex-boyfriends, even those she believed she was in love with, barely crossed her mind after they broke up. Dante was always going to stay with her, no matter where she went.

There was a sizzle when Dante tossed the diced veggies into the hot pan. The sound brought her back. "Penny for your thoughts," he smiled.

"I was just wondering why you decided to cook for me tonight."

"What? I can't impress my girlfriend with my culinary skills?" He flexed and posed while holding the knife.

She shook her head at him. He looked ridiculous. The word girlfriend wasn't lost on her either. "I think you know what I mean," she said.

"Oh. We're cutting to the serious conversation already," he said, slicing the knife through the air. "Are you sure you don't want to wait till dessert?"

"Dante," she said. "C'mon." The jokes were funny, but it was getting them nowhere.

He sighed and put the knife in the sink. "Alright, but I *was* hoping to impress you."

Kat fired another look his way.

"No, I'm serious. I wanted to show I was more than a one trick boyfriend. That I could do more than just open doors and bring you ice cream."

"That's two tricks," Kat pointed out.

He rolled his eyes. "But you're right. I did want to have a chance to talk to you away from the crowds, and the waitresses interrupting our conversation. Just somewhere we weren't going to be distracted by everything going on around us."

"Well, I hope you're going to pay attention to that pan," she said.

"Like I said, I was going to wait until the dessert course." He picked up a large spoon and began stirring the veggies in the pan before dumping two cans of diced tomatoes and a can of tomato paste into it.

While he prepared the marinara sauce, he said, "I know this is only our third date, but I feel like there's something here. Something different than I felt with any other girl I've dated."

"Like what?" Kat asked, knowing the answer. She felt it too.

"This comfort. This feeling like I've known you my whole life. Normally, I'm worried about appearances, how the girl sees me, what she's going to think. What if I trip over my feet and fall flat on my face. With you, I don't worry about it because I know you won't stand there and laugh. You'd help me up."

It melted Kat's heart, not so much because of what he said, but because she felt the same way.

"I don't want to scare you away. I know it's only our third date, and I know we still have a lot to learn about each other. I think at this point with the feelings I have developing for you, if you know you're just going to leave and break my heart, maybe we shouldn't see each other again after tonight."

Kat wasn't sure how to respond to that. This is what she had been afraid of from the start with Dante when he first asked her out. It's what she would've been leery of with anyone who asked her on a date while she was here. Getting attached to someone would make it difficult to leave, and she already knew she would miss him. That was saying a lot considering how little her previous breakups had affected her. Dante was someone she'd never be able to forget.

It hadn't occurred to her he'd just laid his heart on the line for her and was hoping for a better response than silence. When she did speak, he probably wished she had stayed quiet. "So there's no way you'd consider moving to Riverside then?" she asked. It was more a joke to break the tension which had been building over the last few minutes than a serious inquiry.

Kat hadn't expected his answer to be yes. She already knew he wouldn't leave Fogpoint Harbor. All she wanted was a laugh, but she'd settle for a smile. Just some small sign telling her tonight wouldn't be the last time she saw Dante. This town wasn't the life she wanted, but the longer she was around him, the more she realized he was.

There was nothing of the sort in response. His expression dropped as her attempt to joke backfired. Several minutes passed before either of them said anything else. It became so uncomfortable Kat considered pretending to receive a call from Kinley as a means to leave, but she wouldn't do that. If she left now, it was pretty much a certainty they were over.

"Where'd you learn to cook?" Kat asked hoping to break the tension between them.

It was looking like he wasn't going to answer. If she hadn't seen the way his head turned toward her when she spoke, she'd have hoped he just didn't hear her. Kat reached for her phone and fumbled with it, working up the nerve to make it vibrate, so she could say, "I'm sorry. I have to take this."

Dante finally answered her before she got around to it. "You'd think it was my mom, right?" he smiled. "Or my grandma. Some matronly figure in my family. But, you'd be wrong."

He began dishing the food onto plates and carried them to the table. "It was my dad who taught me."

"Really? Your father?" Neither of her parents had ever been worth much in the kitchen. Her dad could make an amazing clam chowder she could devour until the pot was empty. It was a miraculous feat considering her dislike for seafood. There were a few dishes her mom could pull off, but that was it. There was no deciding to try something new in her household. If one of the handful of recipes her parents could handle weren't on the menu, it was frozen food or take out. That's what they practically lived off her whole childhood.

"Yeah," he shrugged. "I guess he was sick a lot when he was growing up. Allergies. He spent most of his free days from school inside which meant he was near his mom in the kitchen."

"Nice," Kat said. "I mean not that he was sick, but that he had that time with her."

"What about you?" he asked. "I take it there wasn't someone showing you around a spice rack when you were a kid."

"No," Kat laughed. "But I did learn a couple things from

my mom."

She took a bite of the penne, and practically moaned in appreciation for it. Pasta had never tasted this heavenly. It was like an award winning soundtrack being played in her mouth.

"Like it?" He beamed as he watched her reaction.

Kat nodded and waited until she swallowed to answer. "Yes, it's delicious."

"Good, I'm glad," he said. "So what did you learn from your mom."

"Well, I learned how to microwave a mean can of ravioli," Kat said. She took another bite of the pasta, trying the chicken with it this time.

Dante chuckled and shook his head. "Seriously, what did she teach you?"

"I'm being serious," Kat insisted, taking another sip of her wine. "That and," she cleared her throat. "Preheat oven to three hundred and fifty degrees, place on cooking sheet in center of the oven, and bake for twelve to fifteen minutes."

He stared at her like she was speaking a foreign language and, to someone who knew how to cook, maybe she was. "You can't cook anything?" he asked in disbelief.

"I wouldn't say that." Kat thought about it. "I mean I can make toast. Kidding!" Although toast was one of her better recipes.

They laughed, and it was finally feeling like things were going back to normal.

"Scrambled eggs, grilled cheese," she continued. "There's a few things I can manage."

"Like French toast?"

Kat shook her head.

"You're joking," he smiled, believing she couldn't be serious.

"No. I had it once," she nodded and looked out of the corner of her eye like she was trying to grasp hold of a memory. "At a restaurant."

"Once? You've had it once?"

She shrugged and sighed. "We didn't go out for breakfast a lot. It was always cereal or oatmeal."

"That's it," he said. Dante walked away from his seat and grabbed something before returning. He plopped a small notepad on the table and began to write. "I'm making a list. Everything you've never ate that you must experience beginning with French toast. It's definitely something you need to try again."

Her mouth dropped. She wasn't sure how serious he was, but his smile relaxed her. Besides, if he was cooking, he could make anything, and she wouldn't complain. If he was planning on making her French toast, it meant he was planning on seeing her again, which meant the night was taking another turn for the better. It never occurred to her in that moment to wonder just how soon he might be fixing her breakfast.

Dante sat across from her poised to write. He stared at her waiting for her to list off more foods she had never tried.

Kat just laughed at him.

"Go on," he said.

It was hard to talk from the near painful grin forming on her face. "I don't know. If I haven't had it, how would I know it's out there to try? I haven't exactly been keeping track of every meal I ever heard about."

"Fair point," he said, pushing the notepad away. "Still, I

want to keep track. There's a world of flavor you've been missing."

She smiled and took another bite. What he said was true. There was more flavor in this one dish than she could remember tasting all year.

After dinner, they took their drinks to the living room and sat on the sofa talking. About nothing. About the past. About everything. The only taboo subject was the future, specifically *their* future. It was like they both understood it had become an unwritten rule at least for tonight. Tomorrow, they might begin anew in failed attempts to sway the other's mind about moving permanently. The only thing written in stone was tonight.

"It's getting late." Kat said for the third time. Dante had picked her up when she could just have easily driven herself. He was out anyway, grabbing something he needed for the meal he'd forgotten.

"It was no trouble," he had said.

Here they were, hours later. Both of them were relaxed and comfortable. Both were aware the night was coming to an end even if they each secretly wished for it to last forever.

He had slipped his shoes off long ago. Kat couldn't quite remember when, but it was after they cozied next to each other. His socked feet were propped on the coffee table, crossed at the ankles.

Dante looked so comfortable. She hated to make him put them back on to drive her home, but he was her ride tonight. It wasn't too appealing for her to get up either. If he scooched out from the corner of the couch and let her lay down, she wouldn't object to sleeping there.

"It is late," he agreed, sitting up.

'*That blew my idea*,' she thought, adjusting herself to sit next to him instead of half on his side.

"But I'm not tired," he said.

He turned to her. His smile made his eyes sparkle with amber specks. It was his smile or the light from the side table. Or, perhaps, the specks were always there waiting for her to find them.

"Do you want to go home?" he asked.

Kat felt like she should know the answer, but she didn't. "Well," she cleared her throat. "I mean... It's late, and I don't want to keep you." She said it as though there was something waiting for Dante in the early morning even though there wasn't.

"But you don't *want* to go," he said, leaning in to her.

She didn't say anything. She didn't breathe. She waited in limbo as time stood still while Dante slowly inched closer until his lips touched hers. A spark jolted through all her senses, and she felt her body come alive in response. This wasn't wrong, but it wasn't smart. She should go, but she wanted to stay.

"Stay," he whispered as if reading her mind.

Kat nodded gently. The movement was so small. It was quiet if movements were measured as decibels, barely able to be discerned, but Dante saw it.

He stood and reached for her hand which she took. Her heart beat quickened, and she found her legs had difficulty remembering how to move for the first few steps she followed him.

By the time they reached his room, her mind was screaming at her to leave. This would make it worse. It would make everything worse. If she thought it was going to be hard to say goodbye now, it would be practically impossible after tonight.

He opened the door and paused, smiling at her again. Kat lifted onto her tip toes and kissed him, letting her mouth find its own way of silencing her mind.

Chapter Twenty-Two
Leave Us Alone

KAT WALKED UP THE STEPS of her porch the next morning. Her movements were awkward and mechanical because she could feel Dante's eyes watching. It seemed odd how having his eyes on her now would affect her like this when he saw all of her last night.

There was a card taped to the door addressed to Katrina Thompson written in horrible chicken scratch. She frowned at the use of her full name. *'It must be from Kinley,'* she thought, tucking it into her purse and fishing for her keys.

She pictured him confused over not getting an answer when he knocked even though her car was in the driveway. Sleeping in was something the man was probably incapable of doing. It made her smile and helped her nerves until she couldn't fit the key into the lock properly and dropped the entire chain of keys on the porch.

Dante's car was still in the driveway where she had exited moments ago. His eyes were still glued to everything she did. It still made her more jittery and hyperaware of every move she made.

Once the door was opened, she rushed inside, closing it behind her and leaning her back against it. She let out a long sigh of relief for having made it in the house without tripping and falling on her face, or something else equally embarrassing.

The car was still idling in the driveway. If he wanted to make sure she made it in the house alright, his work was done. He could leave.

'Was I supposed to do something?' Kat stared at the window nearest to the driveway. Her feet were nailed to the floor, not allowing her to move. *'Should I wave? Is he waiting to see if I look out at him one last time?'*

Back in college, she overheard girls talking about these things all the time. When to call, when not to call, how long to wait before answering a text. It was like dating and finding a good relationship were based more on these key interactions and timing than a connection. If you missed your cue, if you walked onto the stage too soon, the audience would get confused and not understand what was happening with the story. If you were too late, you could miss your chance to shine.

'It was all games,' she thought. *'And they hated for anyone to call it that.'* The boys played them too. It was hard to say who started the game, but everyone played along and knew the rules except for Kat.

She would listen to the girls whisper and plot their agenda. "Don't call him until tomorrow." And never, "If you like him, call him."

The sound of Dante's car was the only thing louder than her heartbeat. It made her wish she had her own team of girls telling her how to handle this situation and exactly what to do.

Kat sighed and grabbed the edge of the curtain, preparing

to give him one last glance when the sound of the engine began to fade. He was backing down the driveway.

Knowing he was leaving, her feet could suddenly move again. She headed up the stairs to take a shower. Kat gasped remembering the way Dante's hand cupped her face so gently.

Tossing her jacket and purse on the bed as she passed, she walked straight into the bathroom. Stepping through the doorway she was taken back to walking into his bedroom, knowing what the night held in store after that point, feeling terrified and excited, having never wanted anything more.

The spray of the water behind her slowly heated to a temperature almost as hot as her blood had been pulsing through her body last night in reaction to his touch. These thoughts would plague her all day if she didn't rein them in now and get control.

After her shower, she wondered what to do with herself for the rest of the day. It was a beautiful day to start clearing out the garage, but she wasn't sure if she wanted to start that project yet.

The only real thing she wanted to do was daydream about Dante. Maybe it could work somehow. Maybe they could compromise. Long distance relationships didn't always fail. If they were the couple who made it, they could start over somewhere new. It didn't have to be in their home towns. As much as she delighted in the idea of spending the day lost in a Neverland which could never be, she needed to get the romantic notions out of her head. They had been doomed from the start. Every second she spent with him was only making the inevitable worse. No one to blame but herself.

Her heart would have her believe another story. Her heart

wanted to move heaven and earth if that's what it took for them to be together. *'But why can't he feel that way about me?'* The negative always takes root stronger than anything. She must care for him far deeper than he returns the affection because he's adamant against giving up anything to make their relationship work. *'I have to stay busy,'* she nodded like she was answering her own question.

"I could always contact Kinley," she muttered out loud. Sadly, he was probably her only friend in Fogpoint not counting Dante. There likely hadn't been an arrest because the news would've spread throughout the town in the blink of an eye. If someone hadn't filled Dante in on the news directly, the talk of the deli they stopped at for breakfast would've been saturated with it.

"Wait." The word came out without effort. Something was lingering in the back of her mind, but wasn't quite coherent. "The card!"

Kat grabbed it from her purse and tore it open. He wouldn't have said anything important in case someone else decided to pry. She was hoping it would say, "I have news. Call me," or something similar.

When she opened it, she stared at it, reading it several times. The outside showed a field of sunflowers. "Leave us alone. You've done enough." Those were the only words scrawled inside the blank card. There was no name attributed to it.

'David,' she thought. *'Has to be.'*

He hadn't been pleased with her from the get. Expecting her to make her way to his shop and have a look around was perhaps already more than he wanted to deal with, and then she showed up at his art show. He'd heard about her visiting the garage where his brother worked. Twice. People had probably made comments and asked questions about if they were suspects which would've worsened his attitude. He wanted her to back off his family.

Kat slid the card back in the envelope and set it on the nightstand, wondering if she should read more into it or not. It could wait until she talked to Kinley again. She didn't believe she was in any real danger.

The card did murder any romanticism she was having about Dante. She threw on her scrubbiest outfit and headed to the garage. With any luck, she wouldn't chance another grazing thought about Dante until she retired for the night, and hopefully, she'd be too exhausted to think.

Kat made fast work of tackling the garage. She'd have enough room to pull her car inside once Sampson was able to make his way out for the next load of junk to sell in his store.

There wasn't a lot to set aside for a more thorough inspection, but there were four decorative photo boxes. Most of the pictures stored inside were in black and white from when her Aunt Dot was a child. She flipped through them quickly and found one of Aunt Dot holding a baby. Something about the photo, the background, seemed off, so she set it aside to look at it closer later. It was probably one she'd seen before. There might be a frame with a duplicate photo inside it in the house. Every surface in every room was lined with pictures.

Most of the photographs she'd wind up keeping. There wasn't much else to do with them except toss them which felt wrong. As she flipped through a few more, she found one of her dad. *'That's odd,'* she thought.

Kat stopped and stared at the peg board wall at the back of the garage. *'Why is it odd?'*

She looked at the picture again. Her dad was buckling the car seat into the car. In the background, she could see the entrance to a hospital. It had been remodeled recently, but she been there enough as a child to recognize it. This was the hospital in Columbia near the little town where she was raised. Her parents always told her that her biological mom was from out of state. Something else didn't add up, but she was lost as to what. *'Why was I at that hospital?'*

'A number of reasons,' she answered her own question.

But that wasn't what struck her as strange. Dot was her dad's aunt. That's what she had been told. *'Then why is this the first picture of him I've ever seen?'*

Kat set the picture aside and pushed the box away. All of the photographs would have to be combed through carefully.

Tossing the stuff she wanted to keep in a box, she headed to the house. There was a lot left to do, and she was getting tired. She needed to get ahold of Sampson and see how soon he could come back. It hit her out of the blue, and she dropped the box just outside the garage door, shattering one of a set of crystal candle holders.

"I wasn't adopted until I was a year old," she said to the front porch. If the ghosts were listening, maybe they could weigh in on it. Her dad shouldn't have been there when she was a baby. "Unless..." she picked up the box and frowned at the broken bits she could see at the bottom.

'Unless there was another baby,' she thought.

Sampson was forgotten in an instant. Kinley might be able to help. She still needed to get ahold of him about the card left on her door. If he couldn't check into her adoption which she suspected, he might be able to point her in the right direction.

With each grand overwhelming thought about the picture and what it meant, she attempted to calm herself. It probably didn't mean anything except she lived with her parents before the adoption. She could've come to them as a foster child. *'Then why didn't they mention it?'*

Her mom had always told her they didn't know her real parents. That was the hospital in Columbia. She set the box on the table in the dining room and carefully pulled the picture back out avoiding the sharp pieces of the candle holder. She barely fit in the car seat. Either side had a bumper made from rolled up blankets to keep her positioned. She couldn't have been more than days old. If she was born in Columbia, she found it impossible to believe her parents didn't know who gave her up. And, it wouldn't be the first lie they told her.

It was a long shot, but the answer might be in this house. Kat closed her eyes and cracked her neck. She should've been more thorough when going through the mounds of junk her aunt had amassed. There could be a letter or document of some kind she saved which might hold a clue, and she hoped it wasn't something she had thrown away already. Everything else would be read twice before tossing it in file thirteen. Once the rest of the junk was gone, she had the better part of a year to spend digging through what was left.

From the corner of her eye, she thought she saw something. A mistake in the layout of the tile in the hallway, but she'd never noticed it before now. Her head tilted to the side as she walked closer to the table with a fresh vase of two day old lilacs sitting on it. There was something on the floor. She bent down and picked it up. It was a card of sorts.

The sound of a car outside made her flush, remembering Dante dropping her off this morning, remembering Dante last night. There was a lot etched into her memory for her to replay in her mind.

She set the card on the table and hurried through the door onto the porch. expecting to find him walking toward the house. The brakes on her feet kicked in so fast she could hear them screech in her mind. It was Kinley.

"Did Ms. Marshall find you?" Kinley asked, walking up the steps.

"What?"

Kat felt out of place like she walked into the wrong theater and didn't know the words for the role she was supposed to play. If Kinley was here, he had information on the case. *'Why is he bringing up Maggie?'*

"So? Did she find you?"

"Maggie?"

Kinley nodded. "I came by this morning. Early. Around eight. But I saw her truck in the driveway. Figured you two had some catching up to do, so I left you to it."

Kat started to look back at the front door then stopped. She could still picture the card taped to it, the one laying on the bedside table in her room. *'Aunt Dot's room.'*

The card was from Maggie which didn't make sense. Being from David, it could be considered some sort of threat, but she at least understood why he left it. There was a reason for it. Kat had only stopped at the farmhouse once and no one was home. She hadn't done anything else to warrant it. *'Maybe someone was home. Someone who didn't want to be bothered by me that day. Or any day it would seem.'*

"I... I never talked to her," Kat said. "I had breakfast with Dante. She must've stopped by then."

"I see. Well, maybe she'll drop back by." he grinned. Kinley cleared his throat. "Are you in the middle of anything? You busy?"

"No, not really," she told him.

"Might I come inside? I think you'll be interested in what I have to say."

Kat pulled the door open and followed Kinley into the front room, but not before glancing down the yard to the cul-de-sac at the end of the street. The mysteries were piling up high enough to replace all the junk she'd cleared out.

Chapter Twenty-Three
Interrogation

KINLEY SAT ON THE EDGE of the sofa with Kat taking the chair adjacent to it and waited. "Would you like something to drink?" she asked, wondering if there was anything besides water in the kitchen.

He shook his head. He was like a young child at Christmas who could barely control his excitement. He rocked slightly forward and back with a grin plastered on his face. It looked like he was about to jump out of his skin if he didn't let loose his news soon.

"Did you get him?" she finally asked.

The grin which was already spread ear to ear somehow managed to grow larger. His eyes twinkled and sparkled like light reflecting off of freshly fallen snow. "Yes." He pumped his fist. Kinley told her the lab delivered the results that morning, and he had stopped by first thing. When he saw the truck, he figured he'd let her be. Family was more important than the case for Kat.

The word family made her stomach flop. Kat had no such thing. She wasn't sure what family actually was anymore.

"How? That surely couldn't be enough evidence," she said.

"No," he agreed. "But it's what we needed to point us in the right direction."

"Did you find the murder weapon?"

"Not yet."

"Did he confess?" There must be something important Kinley hadn't shared yet. She'd watched enough true crime documentaries to know there had to be more than the evidence she found to hold someone. It definitely wasn't enough to charge someone with murder.

"We're bringing him into the station now," Kinley said.

"Then how do you have enough to make an arrest?"

"We don't," he admitted. "Not for the murder. But we have more than enough for other charges. Tampering with evidence. Failure to report a crime. There's negligence charges because he never called for help. There's plenty enough to keep him behind bars while we build our homicide case."

Kinley spun his hat in his hands, looking down at the floor. When he lifted his head, he squinted at the light blindly shining in the room now as the sun came out from behind a cloud. "We couldn't have done it without you, Kat," he said.

Kat shook her head and looked away awkwardly.

"I mean it. You did good."

It was hard for her to take a compliment, always had been. But this? She didn't know what she was doing. This was luck. That and the journal upstairs. If it hadn't pointed her in the right direction, the case would never be solved, not by her input at least. She finally managed a feeble, "Thank you," with a forced smile that probably made Kinley as uncomfortable as she felt.

"You're a natural," he insisted. "It's in your blood."

She nodded slowly not because she agreed, but because she was growing used to being compared to her aunt. He didn't know she and her aunt didn't share the same blood. It couldn't be something in her genes from Aunt Dot, and it wasn't something she picked up by being around her. Coming to Fogpoint for the inheritance was the first she learned of the work her aunt did for the police department.

"Well," he slapped his knee. "I best be getting back to the station. I wanted to stop and personally invite you down there."

"To the station," she asked in surprise, tilting her head to look up at him as he stood.

"Yeah, I thought you might want to watch the interrogation."

"I can do that?" She wasn't entirely sure she wanted to watch, but there was a festering curiosity that longed to follow this through as far as she could. It wasn't like she'd ever have this chance again.

"My personal guest." He smiled at her. "You can ride with me if you'd like."

Kat reached her hand to her head and felt the mess of hair sticking together around her face. "I'm gonna need more than a few minutes to get ready this time," she said.

"Well, hopefully I'll see you soon," he said.

She walked Kinley to the door and caught her reflection in the mirror. Of all the days for a fire to have been lit underneath her to get things done, it had to be today. Her hair was a frizzy, sweaty, cob-webbed mess. Her clothes were dusty. She looked like she hadn't showered in weeks. She wasn't going anywhere looking like this, but she'd have to be quick if she didn't want to miss it.

'*This was exciting,*' Kat thought, racing upstairs to take her second shower of the day. She was covered in dust and cobwebs from working in the garage. It was also a little frightening. Coming that close to a murderer, especially one she helped catch, wasn't going to be easy. She'd already talked to him face to face, but she didn't know for sure what he had done then. Thinking about it made her stomach churn and her knees weak almost to the point of buckling.

Part of her wished she'd taken him up on his offer of a ride. She could've taken a quick shower and been out in five minutes. She was afraid the questioning would be over before she left the house. He might not have been able to wait if she wasn't willing to leave right then. He had said he didn't have much time, but wanted to give her the update in person. How he managed to keep this out of the news and off the town's gossip mill radar was beyond her.

Kat cleaned up and threw on fresh clothes, something more presentable than the scrubby outfit she had been wearing, as quickly as she could. She headed out the door of the bedroom, and as an afterthought, came back and grabbed the note off the nightstand which had been left on the front door. She still wasn't sure if she should mention what it said to Kinley or not, but it wouldn't be this morning. He deserved to enjoy this.

She bounded down the stairs so fast she almost lost her balance and fell. "Wouldn't that be a headline?" she chuckled nervously. "Fogpoint Visitor Cracks Murder Case Wide Open Then Dies After Cracking Open Her Head."

Giving herself a once over at the mirror in the hallway, she couldn't complain too much. This was her personal best record time for getting ready. She tucked the note into her purse and grabbed the picture and card too. There wouldn't be much time to look at them while she was at the station, but she didn't want to forget about them either. Then she was out the door.

Kat arrived at the police station and had no idea where to go. She stood inside the doors and sent Kinley a text, hoping he'd see it before the interrogation began. He might already be in the middle of it, and she'd be out of luck. When she looked up from her phone, a young officer was standing in front of her.

"Miss Thompson?" he asked.

"Yes."

"Kinley's expecting you. Follow me."

He led her down stairs and through a maze of hallways until he stopped in front of a door. "They're expecting you," he said, putting his hand on the door knob.

"Who?" Kat asked. Surely she wasn't going to be sitting in on the interrogation itself.

"Do try to keep your voice down," the officer said. "We're not worried about the suspect hearing you so much, but the others will be trying to listen. And don't worry," he said, opening the door for her. "He can't see you."

When Kat looked inside the room, all she could see was the window on the wall looking in on a room with a small table and chairs set up around it. The room was empty for now. She walked inside and saw three others waiting.

One of the men was dressed in a cheap suit like Kinley and introduced himself as his boss. The chief of police was in full uniform, and the woman who was dressed in a cross between business and stylish, was the mayor. As they introduced themselves, they congratulated her for finding the key piece of evidence needed to solve the case. They thanked her for helping as though her contribution had been voluntary, and she wasn't just doing what the department hired her to do.

They waited for what felt like an eternity. Kat leaned against the wall in the back corner of the room, forcing herself to keep her eyes off her watch. Her hair was still wet, making the back of her shirt damp. Turns out she had plenty enough time to dry it, but had been worried about taking too long. *'Hurry up and wait,'* she thought.

Their attention turned to the window, and Kat could see the door in the adjoining room had opened. One by one walked in Kinley and another detective she didn't recognize. They were followed by a tall skinny man in a suit too wide for his frame. He were glasses atop of his large nose and was balding on top of his head. The comb over did little to cover the round patch of skin underneath. After them, Harold's grandson was led into the room by a uniformed officer.

Even though Kat knew he couldn't see her, she still held her breath when he walked into the interrogation room. He was almost unrecognizable, a hollowed out shell of his former self. He took a seat next to his lawyer, and Kinley got underway. She barely paid attention to what was being said as the detectives asked a few questions to verify his personal information. Her primary focus was on him and his behavior. Some of the interrogation did catch her attention, but she wasn't following closely.

"Were you at your grandfather's house the evening he died?" Sergeant Taylor asked.

"No."

"You weren't?" The sergeant acted surprised by the answer. "We have evidence linking you to the scene. We know you removed something from the hallway."

His eyes were red and puffy as though he'd been crying, probably more from the reality of being caught than from any remorse one might hope he felt. His eyes were lost, two empty beads sunken into his head.

"Earlier that day, yeah, I stopped by."

"When was this?" Kinley asked.

He shrugged his shoulders. "I don't know."

"You don't know?" Kinley asked.

"I'm not sure. That afternoon I think."

His lawyer said something Kat didn't catch, and he nodded, looking almost relieved. It was followed by a brief moment when he looked calmer and relaxed, confident in himself and the proceedings. Then the sergeant spoke again.

"Just talk to us," the sergeant said. "We know what you removed was covered in blood, your grandfather's blood. That's why you're here. You were at his house between his attack and when the maid found his body in the morning."

His body slumped, depressed and exhausted. It was the look of defeat. He didn't answer.

"Why didn't you call for help?" Kinley asked.

He shook his head. The unforgiving lights in the little room where he sat reflected off his eyes like a sparkling sea. He was beginning to cry again.

"You wanted your grandfather to die, didn't you? That's why you didn't call for help." Sergeant Taylor's voice was loud. There was no chance Kat could miss hearing it. "Did you attack your grandfather?"

"Don't answer that," his lawyer advised. The lawyer said something to the two detectives, but Taylor was standing now in front of the lawyer. The voices were muffled, and Kat could only make out a couple words.

"...bleeding at the bottom of the stairs," Kinley was saying.

Kat had been so focused on his eyes that she wasn't following the questioning again. They were dull and lackluster, having lost their life, their arrogance, their disdain for people he felt were beneath him which seemed to be endless. They had lost everything which had once defined him until they were empty voids.

"...money..."

She caught something the sergeant was saying. He was accusing him of killing his grandfather for the inheritance. It wouldn't be the first time someone looking to collect insurance or an estate murdered a family member. It was a tale as old as time. Money will drive people to great lengths. *'Like live in a haunted house for a year.'*

"He wouldn't give you any more money, would he?" Kinley asked. "How many times has he bailed you out? Failed businesses. Wrecked cars. Wasn't there an issue a few years back with a girlfriend who needed to go to the city for a uh... medical procedure?"

The lawyer intervened again. The three men raised their voices briefly then it was over. Harold's grandson was being led out and taken back to his cell. His lawyer had declared their questioning over.

Whether he'd ever admit his guilt or not, his face wore all the admission Kat needed to see. Almost as if he could read her mind, he burst into sobs, turning his head to the side trying to bury his face into his shoulder, unable to use his hands.

There were murmurs from the other officers around her in the room, but she was lost on what had happened. Bits and pieces of the interrogation floated around in her mind, but not enough to make sense of it. The door opened and Detective Kinley stood there.

When he saw her, he lifted up his hands and clapped. "It's all because of you, Kat," he said.

The others in the room joined him and said things like, "Good job," before walking into the hall where they talked to the sergeant and each other.

She shook her head. "I barely did anything."

"You gave us what we needed to get him." Kinley turned toward the wall facing the now empty interrogation room then glanced into the hallway at his peers. He nodded and waved at one of them. "And we did get him, Kat," he said.

Someone new was standing near the mayor and motioning to Kinley to join them. "Give me a minute," he said.

"Oh. Yeah, go," Kat said, watching the growing commotion in the hallway.

Kinley walked out the door and joined the others. Their spirits were high, and they were talking about the murder case they still needed to build. She hung back in the darkened room by herself watching from a distance. This wasn't her victory regardless of how much credit they gave her. It was a little overwhelming, and she wondered if she'd ever get used to it.

Chapter Twenty-Four
Weekend Plans

KAT SET THE TRAY ON the table in the hallway and tucked a tendril of hair that had fallen into her face behind her ear. She reached into her purse and pulled out the card she found on the floor days ago. It was an old birth announcement. The baby in the photograph was not happy. Her face was flushed deep red and scrunched so tightly her eyes were two barely discernable slits. Her mouth was open wide, and her two tiny hands were curled into fists. Her wail could still be heard by looking at the picture.

None of the fields under the picture had been filled out. The lines for birthdate, time, and length and weight were empty. The baby could've belonged to anyone her aunt had known over the years, but something in her gut told Kat the baby was important.

It wasn't Jillian although she was the only one in Aunt Dot's family young enough to have a colorized baby picture. Kat had come across a number of photos from Jillian's childhood. She had been born bald and didn't sprout more than a couple small wisps of light blonde hair until she was several months old. A mass of thick dark hair clung tightly to the baby's head in this announcement.

One of the boards on the porch creaked under Dante's weight and brought her attention back to what she was supposed to be doing. She dropped the card in her purse, checked her hair once more, and picked up the tray. She balanced it carefully as she opened the door, and Dante quickly came to help.

He put it on the table between their chairs, pouring each of them a glass of lemonade. It was a rather warm day for autumn. It was one of the last ones they'd have before autumn's grip took hold and turned into winter. *'I could get used to this,'* she thought, feeling the security in Dante's smile. It had been on her mind a lot in the week since the arrest.

"How did you know?" Dante asked. "I've been wondering about that. How could you tell it was blood and not paint splattered on that painting?"

Kat shrugged her shoulders and shook her head.

"Don't do that," he said.

"What?"

"Don't play it off like it's nothing. You did this, Kat. You."

When Kinley and the other detectives praised her, it made her a little uncomfortable. She didn't feel like she had done much. It was luck. But when Dante did it, she felt capable and made her feel good about herself.

"Well," she said, "we knew something was taken from the scene. A painting had always been a possibility given Harold's surprising collection and the shape of the object." It could've been anything rectangular in shape though.

While she was at his art show, many people were

whispering behind David's back. They were surprised he was opening another studio in the city when this one was bleeding money. His grandfather Harold had been funding every one of David's ventures. She had thought the blood splatter was paint at first until she stepped back, and the specks of blood illuminated under the light. In her mind, she could see the painting leaning against the wall in the hallway at the top of the stairs with the spray of blood lining up perfectly. "It was a hunch more than anything."

"It was a good one," Dante smiled.

They sipped their drinks and enjoyed the quiet. In the spring, Kat planned on fixing a few things in the sunroom style back porch, maybe adding a swing so she could watch the wildlife romp and play among the trees.

The driveway looked strange with only Dante's car parked on it. The garage was empty now, and Kat could pull her car inside. Her real work at the house was done. Anything else she did to improve it was extra. Everything had been cleared out, but it still didn't feel like a home. It was her aunt's house, restored to the way she remembered it when she used to visit as a child. It would always feel like Aunt Dot's house until she made it her own.

'But they say home is where the heart is.' She looked at Dante.

"He denied it for so long. What made him finally confess?" he asked, unaware Kat was changing the topic in her mind.

"It was when they found the finial. His fingerprints and his grandfather's DNA were on it," she said. The moment they showed it to him David lost it. The reality of what he'd done hit hard when he had to face it. Murdering his grandfather wasn't something he'd planned. David was angry, and when the finial came off in his hand, he hit his grandfather without thinking about what he was doing.

"Did he say why he did it?"

Kat nodded and inhaled deeply. "Harold wasn't going to give him any more money."

He had supported David longer than was reasonable. His grandson had every opportunity to give his dreams a good chance. He believed it was time for David to find a more sustaining line of work like utilizing his teaching degree.

According to Adam, there was an agreement David had made with their grandfather after he graduated college. Harold would help him out, give him the loan he needed to open his studio, but it didn't end there. His grandfather pumped money into the studio many times to save it from closure. After he started the painting classes, it was finally breaking even. That's when David came up with the idea that a studio in the city would be more lucrative, and he wanted his grandfather's help with it too.

"It's supposed to be warm this weekend," Dante said, changing the subject. "Is there anything you had in mind?"

Kat wasn't sure why it had been such a hard decision, why she was so adamant against it. There was nothing for her back home. She had left her job and gave up her apartment. The few friends she managed to stay in touch with since college had barely called since she came to Fogpoint, and she hadn't heard from any of them in weeks. There was nothing for her there except a storage unit filled with the contents of her old place. She'd have to start over again regardless of where she lived.

"I have to make a trip down to Riverside actually. Wanna

come?"

Dante thought it over. "Sure. What do you have going on there?"

"I have a storage unit I need to clear out."

His eyes widened and he started to say something but stopped. Finally, he simply asked, "Really?"

Kat grinned and nodded at him.

Later that evening, Kat was getting ready for bed. The last words Dante spoke to her before leaving, "I love you," played on repeat in her head. She sat at the desk with the journal open thinking about the new life she was about to begin. There were still a ton of questions to answer, mysteries to solve. Who was the baby in the announcement? Did Jillian have a child? Why does Maggie want nothing to do with her? What was this agreement her parents had with Aunt Dot and why? She wondered if she'd ever get to the bottom of all of it.

Before she switched the desk lamp off to head to bed, she looked down at the journal. Scrawled across the page it read, "Kat holds the answer."

More by Jennifer Lush

Available everywhere in eBook,
Paperback, and on Kindle Vella

The Elementals Series

Air

Earth

Fire

Water

Balance

Ravenwood

Volumes One and Two

The Below: Phillipe's Revenge

The Below: Mezzie's Prison

Fogpoint Harbor

The Inheritance

Buried Secrets
The Sacrificial Dagger
Line of Sight

About the Author

JENNIFER LUSH IS A mother of three from central Illinois where she has lived her entire life. Aside from spending time with her children and grandchildren, writing and traveling are her two main consuming passions. Luckily, they are mutually beneficial.

Writing has always been in her blood even if it took her longer than planned to do it. One of her earliest memories of longing to be an author happened in kindergarten when she told her parents what she wanted to be when she grew up. It took close to four decades, but she has finally made that childhood dream come true.

Jennifer is an entertainer at heart who is always making those around her laugh. She can turn any mundane event into a story worth repeating with flair. Inspiration for her fictional worlds comes from everywhere. There are more ideas floating through her mind than she has time to write, but she is determined to finish as many as possible.

Twitter: AuthorJLush
IG: AuthorJenniferLush
Tik Tok: AuthorJenniferLush